flavor of the week

by

tucker shaw

HYPERION PAPERBACKS
New York

ACKNOWLEDGMENTS

Big thanks to Judy Goldschmidt, Ben Schrank, and Eloise
Flood. To Alessandra Balzer, Josh Bank, Leslie Morgenstein,
Lauren Monchik, Jennifer Blanc, and Amy Beadle. Thanks to
Susan Kaplow. To everyone at Alloy. Many, many thanks to
Jorge, Danny, and Luiz.

Produced by 17th Street Productions,
an Alloy company
151 West 26th Street
New York, NY 10001

First American Paperback edition, 2005
Printed in the United States of America
  3 5 7 9 10 8 6 4 2
Library of Congress Cataloging-in-Publication Data on file.
ISBN 0-7868-5698-X
Visit www.hyperionteens.com

For Gramp—here's hoping you're holding
court in the kitchen next time we meet

kitchen-sink cookies

"It's okay, Mom. Don't worry. Everyone will be gone by midnight," Cyril Bartholomew said. He hoped it was true. "We're hardly spending any money, and besides, I got paid today. Okay?"

"All right," Mrs. Bartholomew said. "Listen, I'm being paged to the ER. I have to run." She hung up, and Cyril went back to work. He had a party to throw for Rose Mulligan.

Rose was his lab partner and the most beautiful girl on the planet. Cyril was cross-eyed in love with her—he'd throw himself off a cliff for her. He'd even starve. Except she didn't know it. Not yet.

He rolled a ball of uncooked dough in his mouth and savored the buttery sweetness, then he slid the sheet of perfectly spaced cookie-dough balls into the ancient iron oven and wished he were really cooking for Rose. In reality, he was cooking for Rose's friend Jamie and twenty or thirty of her closest friends. It was Jamie's birthday, and Cyril had offered to have a party for her at his house as an excuse to spend more time with his beloved. If Cyril were actually cooking for Rose, he'd only be cooking for two, and he wouldn't be baking kitchen-sink cookies. He'd prepare an elegant, romantic dinner, candles and all. And he'd call it Aphrodisia. Aphrodisia would begin with ice-cold, freshly shucked oysters rising plump and firm from their shells. Little dollops of horseradish would balance on top of the oysters, and they'd glisten with squeezed lemon. No, wait. Oysters wouldn't work. Rose, God bless her kind, crunchy-granola, patchouli-wearing, peace-love-and-understanding soul, was a vegetarian. Aphrodisia would begin as a platter of figs, dusted with spices, mild and sweet. Then golden flatbreads with savory dips and sauces and slathers. There would be artichokes, dunked in melted butter. And for the pièce de résistance, rich, creamy bonbons, oozing with molten chocolate. The scents of vanilla and ginger and nutmeg would swirl around them like music in the amber light. And when the meal was over, her perfect lips would taste as sweet as——

Well, Cyril never got that far. The egg-shaped kitchen timer went off before he and Rose could kiss. Cyril opened his eyes and pushed a blond lock out of his face. He wasn't making Aphrodisia today. In fact, the chances of Aphrodisia really ever happening were as fat as Cyril was—and all 240 pounds of him knew it. Sure, he and Rose were friends. But she was way out of his league.

As Cyril started assembling the next sheet of dough balls, he heard a voice come from the backyard.

"Cyril?" It was Rose! Cyril's heart sped up and he sprang to the back door, slapping flour dust out of his jeans.

"Hey! You're early!" He pushed at the screen door, which squeaked and groaned like every respectable upstate New York screen door, and a sloppy-ponytailed Rose stepped halfway in. She balanced a big box of birthday decorations on her forearms while clutching her keys and cell phone in her hand.

"How's it going?" Rose said breathlessly. Halfway through the door, glasses creeping down her nose, she spun around. "Simon! Garfunkel! Here, boys!" Moments later her two cocker spaniels scurried between her legs and into the kitchen, toes clicking on the terra-cotta floor. "I love birthday parties. I'm so glad I finally convinced Jamie to let us throw her one! She kept saying she wasn't

3

in a party mood this year, but whatever. *Everyone* wants a party on their birthday."

Rose set the box on the counter, pushed her glasses back onto her perfect nose, and deftly pulled her chestnut ponytail perfectly neat and tight. Cyril felt like he was in the presence of a girl who'd just transformed herself into a goddess.

"Don't you think? I mean, you love parties, don't you?" asked the goddess.

Cyril smiled and his stomach fluttered. He had dreams about her ponytail. He could watch her fix her ponytail forever. "Yeah," he answered, not exactly sure what the question was.

"Yes, she needs a party. No doubt." Rose closed her eyes and inhaled dramatically. "Mmm. What's that smell?" She smoothed out her tie-dyed T-shirt, one of Cyril's favorites. Actually, Cyril loved all of her clothes.

"Uh, it's, uh, cookies." Cyril's eyes darted to Rose's clogs, then back to his own navy blue Converse One Stars. "I'm kind of, like, watching them. For my ... uh ... mother."

Nice save, Bartholomew.

Rose's shining brown eyes smiled an instant before her mouth joined in. "Don't tease me, now. Do you know what the sight of a boy in the kitchen *does* to a girl?" Cyril was spellbound at the way she sparkled. But he was also partly busy mentally kicking himself for not finishing the cookies before Rose came over. He preferred to keep his cooking a secret. It wasn't that he was *embarrassed* about it. He'd been happily feeding his family for years. By the time he was thirteen, hardly anyone else in his family even *entered* the kitchen. It was Cyril's domain. In fact, he planned to become a professional chef once he graduated from the legendary American Institute of Culinary Arts, the most rigorous, intense, cutthroat, and best cooking school in the country, which happened to be right up the road. It was just that talking about cooking with anybody outside his family got too terribly close to talking about his weight. And that was a conversation Cyril did not want to have.

Luckily, just then Rose's phone began to vibrate, buzzing across the kitchen counter and almost toppling to the ground. Rose dove for it and glanced at the readout. "It's Jamie," she muttered. "She better not be freaking out about this party again." Rose put the phone to her ear. "Hello?"

Cyril watched Rose struggle to get a word in, but all she could manage on her end of the conversation was, "Oh no . . . Jamie, that sucks. . . . He's just a big loser, that's all. . . . No, I understand. It's okay. . . . Of course I'm

5

not mad. It's okay. . . . Yes . . . Okay, call later . . . Bye."
She clicked off her phone and rolled her eyes at Cyril. "I
can't believe it, after inviting everyone I could think of,
this loser she's been dating—*Alfred from Vassar*, I mean,
what kind of name is Alfred, anyway?—this loser dumps
her on her birthday. See, that's exactly why I'm staying
away from guys because that's what they always do—and
now she doesn't want a birthday party."

"So, now what?" Cyril didn't really care that much
about the party, but he was looking forward to spending all afternoon and evening with Rose. Even if she
was staying away from guys.

"I can't believe it! *Alfred from Vassar.*"

Cyril could have listened to Rose saying "Alfred
from Vassar" in that mocking singsong tone for days.

"She says she can't go through with it." Rose gave
her phone the finger. "I hate him." Cyril figured Rose
meant Alfred, not the phone.

Ah, sweet, quirky Rose. The girl who was sparkling
a minute ago now collapsed across the couch, limp, like
she'd been unplugged. Her lights had gone out, and
Cyril wanted to turn them back on. "Rose?"

"I guess I'd better start calling people and telling
them the party's off." She fluttered her lashes and rolled

6

her beautiful eyes at Cyril. She reached for her phone.

"Wait," he said, stroking his chin. "Listen, don't call anyone. Look. Moms is already on the graveyard shift at the hospital. And Dad, well, Dad's never home. And you already bought the festive paper cups. It's party time, Rose. We'll just make it a party-party instead of a Jamie party."

"Really?" The lights flickered, but Rose sounded unsure. She stood up from the couch and walked over to Cyril.

"Yeah. Why not?"

"You're so right. Why shouldn't we have a party? Cyril, I could kiss you!" And before he knew what was happening, she grabbed him by the ears and did exactly that, right on the lips. "You *rule!*"

Cyril could feel himself turning purple as his crystal blue eyes widened.

"Want a cookie?" he asked, and then he kept quiet before his voice totally cracked. Nice save again.

But by the time he could reach over to grab one, the screen door was squealing shut and Rose was halfway to her car. She laughed and yelled out, "I've got to go get dressed! See you later."

She managed to stay a step ahead of the dogs, who yapped at each other in her trail of light.

1¾ cups all-purpose flour

1 teaspoon fresh baking soda

½ teaspoon salt

2 sticks unsalted butter, softened

1¼ cups firmly packed brown sugar. Light or dark.

2 large fresh eggs

¼ teaspoon fresh ground nutmeg

2 teaspoons whole milk

3 teaspoons real vanilla extract. Not imitation, ever.

2 cups uncooked old-fashioned rolled oats

1 cup semisweet chocolate chips

1–2 cups of Reese's pieces, coconut flakes, walnuts, M&M's, or whatever else you feel like

1. Preheat oven to 375 degrees Fahrenheit.
2. Get all your ingredients organized. Make sure you have everything.
3. In a medium bowl whisk together the flour, baking soda, and salt.
4. In a large bowl with electric mixer, beat the butter and sugar on medium speed until creamy, about 2 minutes.
5. In a smaller bowl gently beat the eggs with a fork to break up yolks.
6. Add the nutmeg, eggs, milk, and vanilla to the butter mixture; beat on medium for another minute until color is even and texture is consistent.

kitchen-sink cookies

7. Add the flour mixture to the butter mixture; mix at medium speed until blended.

8. Fold in all the good stuff: oats, chocolate chips, coconut, nuts, whatever. Do this gently. Don't overwork the dough, don't overmix. In fact, undermix.

9. Drop dough by big fat rounded tablespoonfuls onto ungreased cookie sheets lined with parchment paper, waxed paper, or a Silpat liner. (Don't worry about putting parchment paper or waxed paper in the oven. It won't catch on fire or anything like that.)

10. Bake 9–10 minutes in the middle of the oven. Bake only one sheet at a time, so cookies bake evenly. It takes longer this way, but it's worth it.

11. Cool 1–2 minutes on cookie sheets; then remove to wire rack.

12. Eat. If there are any left, store them tightly covered at room temperature.

Makes two to three dozen cookies

rhubarb iced tea

"You mean there are more people coming? What did you do, post it on the Web?" Cyril was teasing, but he was also surprised. He'd never seen this many people in his backyard before. It was only nine-thirty, but at least thirty-five New Hyde Park Regional High School students were milling around, slurping iced tea and munching bread sticks and chicken wings in the perfect September evening.

"Well, not really." Rose sipped her iced tea while smiling across the picnic table at Cyril. "But I did send an invite to everyone in my address book."

Cyril smiled back, shaking his head. "Well, that explains it. You have the biggest address book at New Hyde. You're the only person I know who is friends

10

with the popular kids, and the burnouts, *and* the fringe people. Hell, if it weren't for you, I don't think I'd ever end up at the same party as Brandon Keifler."

Rose gasped. "He's here? How dare he? I didn't even invite him!" Brandon Keifler was the overgrown, letter-jacketed, prep-turned-meathead who'd broken Rose's heart two weeks earlier.

"Is he coming this way?" Rose asked. "I knew I shouldn't have worn my glasses!"

"Not yet. And you're wrong about the glasses. I love the way you look in them," answered Cyril, and he meant it.

"You do?" Rose smiled at him, sliding her glasses back on her nose. "So do I. But no one else gets why I wear them. Jamie tells me to just wear contacts." She looked across the crowd. "Okay, no more Brandon talk. How 'bout all this food? Where did you get it all, any-way?" she asked. "Everyone's talking about the cookies."

"Oh yeah? You want one?" Cyril pushed a plate piled high with kitchen-sinks across the table toward Rose.

"Not now. I have that nervous party feeling. Maybe later," said Rose. "But say thanks to your mother or whoever made them."

Cyril ate a cookie, and then his mouth was too full

to say the truth. Rose took another sip of iced tea. "What's in this tea?" she asked. "It's sooo good!"

"I think it's rhubarb," said Cyril.

"Nope, it's not rhubarb," said Rose, sipping again. "I think it's raspberry or something. Hey, have you seen Jamie?"

"Actually, I'm pretty sure it's—" Cyril stopped himself just short of correcting her and giving himself away. Who knew lying was such hard work? "I mean, I'm pretty sure *she's* with Trent Dufresne."

"No way! Well, it's a good thing we didn't throw her a birthday party or anything. We wouldn't have wanted her to forget about *Alfred* too quickly." Rose laughed, shaking her head. Rose didn't care that Jamie was a little—what's the word—easy. To her a friend was a friend. "Where are they?"

"I'm pretty sure they're in your car."

"No *way!*" Rose paused; sipped. "Well, good for them. Here's to Jamie!"

"To Jamie," echoed Cyril.

They clinked iced-tea glasses, and Rose continued. "I don't know what she sees in him. Actually, I don't know what she sees in any guy. Personally, I'm through with them. At least for a while. They all suck." Rose made a gagging motion, then looked up at Cyril. "Present company excluded, of course. I'm talking about boyfriend-type guys, not friend-friend-type guys. Not you, Cyril."

Just the sound of her words made Cyril's intestines do a 360-degree turn. But he couldn't let Rose know that. He had to play it cool. Luckily, he had more pressing business to attend to.

"Uh, speak of the devil."

"Don't tell me." Now Rose looked like *her* intestines were doing a 360.

"Yes," said Cyril, lowering his voice to a heavy whisper and his eyebrows to a heavy furl. "It is he who must not be named."

"No!" Rose dropped her head to the table. "Isn't it bad enough that he's here? Does he have to come over and talk to me?"

Before either one of them could continue the conversation, Brandon approached the picnic table. An unidentified frosted blonde with frosted lips hung off him, and she was looking very grateful. Cyril wondered if she thought Brandon had just liberated her people or something.

"Hi, Rose." His voice was way too tinny and small

for the size of his body. Cyril noticed that this happened to a lot of guys who lifted too many weights, and it gave him a spike of satisfaction.

Rose picked up her head and smiled back, tense. "Hi." She turned to his date. "I'm Rose." Before even shaking the girl's hand, Rose turned to Cyril. "Cyril, I'm going to find Jamie." Rose stood up, adjusted her ponytail, and was gone, making a beeline for the house.

Cyril turned to Brandon and his date. "Grab some cookies before they're gone," he said before launching himself after Rose, iced teas in hand.

Rose was rounding the side of the house, headed for Shingle Camp Hill Road, when Cyril caught up with her.

"Rose! Wait! Hey!" Cyril said, sounding out of breath. "You okay?" he said with a big exhale as he fell into her stride.

"Whatever, no big deal. I just don't do well with Brandon Keifler in my face." Rose kept walking, away from the light of the house.

"How could anyone do well with Brandon Keifler in their face? I mean, he's on the other side of the house and I can smell him from here." Rose giggled as Cyril handed over her iced tea.

"Mademoiselle, your tea?"

"His date is overfrosted," Rose continued.

"She's a walking Mini-Wheat," he said.

Rose loved it when Cyril agreed with her. It made his blue eyes look even bluer.

"She's like a *before* picture for a makeunder," she deadpanned.

"*Perfect* for Brandon," Cyril added.

If Cyril were any other guy, Rose might not have felt so comfortable bitching to him about Brandon. Guys tended to think girls were catty when they bitched instead of just human—like guys never bitched themselves. But Cyril was so accepting. He just *got* it.

Rose gave Cyril's elbow a squeeze. "Why aren't there more guys like you?" she asked.

But Cyril, who seemed distracted by the sound of a dog barking in the background, didn't answer back.

"No way," Cyril muttered, spinning around to look up the road. "Mandy?" He turned back to Rose, shaking his head. "Sorry, I thought I knew that bark. This dog that used to live here. But it couldn't be her. What were you saying?"

Before Rose could respond, a big, beautiful chocolate Lab leaped out from between the parked cars and onto

Cyril's feet, tongue and tail wagging in sync. "Mandy?" Cyril knelt down, steadying himself with one arm. "Mandy! What are you doing here?" He stood back up. "This is *so* weird. This *is* Mandy. She used to live up the road. I thought she moved to New York City with Nick."

Rose fell in love with Mandy at first sight. She was absolutely adorable. Rose crouched down next to her to stroke her neck. "You're gorgeous! Simon and Garfunkel would *love* you." She scratched Mandy's ears and looked up at Cyril. "Who's Nick?"

"Oh, just this guy who lived next door. Was kinda like my best friend."

"*Kinda* like your best friend?" asked Rose. "But you've never even mentioned him before."

Suddenly Cyril got all twitchy. "Um, yeah, well, he moved to Manhattan to live with his uncle two years ago and never said good-bye, so I wasn't sure what was up. I knew that his dad moved to England to be a fancy lawyer and that his mom was pretty upset about the whole thing. I figured maybe he didn't want to talk about it."

"You guys never talked about it?" Rose asked.

"His mom was always on his case. So I didn't want be just another person who was on his case, ya know?"

Actually, Rose didn't know. Maybe it was a girl thing,

16

but if Jamie ever left town without saying good-bye, Rose would be beside herself. Further evidence that guys and girls were probably never meant to be together.

As an approaching shadow turned into a runner, Rose was forced to abandon her thoughts.

"Mandy!" yelled the runner as he came into the light. "Mandy! Come here, girl!"

"Who's that?" asked Rose as Mandy barked.

"I can't believe it," muttered Cyril. "It's Nick."

The runner, no longer a shadow now, was upon them, noisy track jacket swish-swooshing with each slowing stride. "Hey, man," he called, lunging for Cyril and pulling him in for a hug.

"Good Lord, it's been a long time!"

Good Lord was right. As in, the good Lord must have created this beautiful six-footer with her bare hands. He was gorgeous. Breathtaking. Stunning. *And* he had blue eyes, Rose's favorite. And thick wavy brown hair that grazed his shoulders, Rose's other favorite.

Cyril broke from Nick's grip just long enough to get another look at him, then pulled him in again. "Good Lord."

"You already said that," said Rose and Nick in unison. Then they laughed in unison. Rose gave Nick the quickest once-over she could squeeze in without getting busted.

"Uh, Cyril?" said Rose, whose eyes were locked on Nick's face. "Aren't you going to introduce us?"

"Right. Of course. Rose Mulligan, this is Nick Garbacchio. Nick, this is Rose." Cyril said it so quickly, it was as if he were being graded for speed. "Dude, what are you doing here?"

"Hi, Rose," said Nick. "Very nice to meet you."

"Nice to meet you, too, Nick," said Rose, shaking his hand. She could feel her face and neck turning pink and hoped that it was too dark out for Nick to notice. "I don't think I remember you," said Nick, hand still closed around Rose's. She prayed he'd never let go.

Rose laughed. "Oh, I moved here a couple of years ago. It feels like forever." She was batting her eyelashes, which was way over the top, but she couldn't make herself act normal.

"Okay, so you two never met before," said Cyril.

What's his rush? Rose wondered. Shouldn't Cyril be trying to help her get to know his friend? Then again, Rose had been pretty down on guys lately, so maybe keeping her away from Nick *was* Cyril's way of helping. Thank goodness for Cyril and his levelheadedness.

"Nick, what are you doing here? What's going on? How long are you here for? What's with the jogging?" Cyril asked.

"Oh, this. I'm training for the cross-country team now," said Nick. He was still holding Rose's hand, and Rose was still letting him. "At New Hyde Park Regional. I'm a couple of weeks late, but I start classes on Monday."

"What? What are you talking about? What about New York?" asked Cyril.

"I mean I moved back. I'm back!" Nick looked at Cyril. "We're neighbors again, man!" He dropped Rose's hand and grabbed Cyril around the neck. "Just like back in the day! Sweet, huh!"

"Dude, that's awesome!"

No kidding that's awesome, Rose thought.

Still holding on to Cyril, Nick looked back at Rose. "Do you go to New Hyde?"

"Yeah," said Rose. "I do."

"I hope we have some classes together," said Nick, grinning.

"Me too," said Rose, hoping that Nick would pick up her hand again. He didn't. But Cyril did invite him over to the party, and he accepted, so maybe there'd be time for some more hand-holding later.

Just then Jamie came walking toward the three-some, looking as sultry as ever, her shiny ringlets of black hair bouncing with each step she took. Rose couldn't remember ever feeling so unhappy to see her.

"Jamie!" Cyril said, practically squealing. Rose had never seen Cyril get so enthusiastic over Jamie. "Where have you been?"

"Nowhere special." Jamie smirked, rubbing the corners of her mouth. "But Trent says hi." She tucked her waffle-weave undershirt with the Harley's Angels logo into her low-rise jeans and smiled at Nick. Rose could swear Jamie was sticking out her chest. "I'm Jamie. Who are you?" asked Jamie as she held out her hand.

"I'm Nick. Nice T-shirt."

Is he going to hold her *hand now?*

"Thanks," said Jamie as she looked Nick up and down. "Nice legs. What are you, some kind of runner?"

Okay, missy; now, that's enough.

Rose was overwhelmed. It had been only two weeks since Brandon had dumped her, two weeks since she had decided to go off boys for a while. And here she was, already getting bent out of shape over a guy she had met less than two minutes ago. She definitely needed a time-out.

"Jamie, can I talk to you for a second?" Rose asked, trying to sound as edgeless as possible. "In the bathroom?"

"Sure, Rosie," said Jamie, frowning. "What's wrong?"

"Nothing, I just need to talk to you. Are you done with Trent?"

"Rosie, even if I weren't done, you know I'd ditch him for you." Jamie put her arm around Rose.

"Uh, hey, guys . . . I hate to interrupt this Hallmark moment, but we have a party going on," said Cyril. "Shall we?" He motioned toward the house.

"We shall, Cyril." Rose smiled at him, then took Jamie's arm. "I just have to ask Jamie a question, and then it's party time."

"What question?" Jamie asked as they walked off.

Rose waited until she entered the bathroom to answer her. She lowered the toilet lid and plunked herself down on top of it.

"Jamie, I'm all over the place. I don't know if it's because I just saw Brandon— "

"Or if it's because that Nick guy is so damn cute . . ." Jamie interrupted as she sidled up onto the sink.

Rose could tell by the way Jamie was swinging her legs that she was eager to deconstruct the greatness of

Nick, but Rose had no desire to go there. She was afraid of putting her feelings for Nick into words. At the same time, she didn't want to validate Jamie's feelings for him, either. Basically, she wasn't ready for Nick to exist.

"I guess," Rose said dismissively. "Whatever it is, I just want to stay away from guys for a little while longer. So, would you consider being my date for the homecoming dance?"

"Sure," said Jamie as she sniffed under her arm to make sure her deodorant was still working. "But don't be so sure that going as each other's dates will keep the guys away. It might make us more irresistible."

Rose felt a wave of relief. As long as she kept Jamie and Cyril close to her side, she was safe from the evils of boys. For now, anyway.

8–10 good-sized stalks fresh red rhubarb

½ cup sugar

4 herbal tea bags (mint, lemon, or berry . . . choose something sweet)

3 quarts cold water

1. Chop up the stalks of rhubarb into pieces about the size of your thumb. Wash them thoroughly.
2. Drop the rhubarb into a large pot with the cold water. Bring to a boil over high heat, then turn heat down to medium low, cover, and simmer for 45 minutes to 1 hour. Uncover and let cool for at least 15 minutes.
3. Put the sugar and tea bags into a large glass iced-tea pitcher.
4. Pour the rhubarb water through a sieve into the pitcher, making sure rhubarb pieces don't end up in the tea. Let tea sit and steep for half a day. Remove tea bags.
5. Pour the tea into a glass filled to the rim with ice. Add mint leaves or a slice of lemon.

Makes about twelve glasses

late-night bacon and eggs

Those kids from Rose's address book sure knew how to party. It took Cyril, Nick, Rose, and Jamie an hour and a half to clean up after them. But by two Nick was home and Rose and Jamie were at Denny's to postmortem the party. Cyril had no trouble picturing the girls discussing Trent the hottie, Brandon the jerk, even Nick the new guy . . . everyone but Cyril the non–"boyfriend type."

It stung. But Cyril could take it. He'd been the biggest kid in school for as long as he could remember, and he knew all about disappointment. He knew how to intercept it before it took hold, how to stuff it away, to banish it from sight, to swallow it. He even knew what to eat to kill the aftertaste.

He started loading the dishwasher, slowly, and didn't even flinch when he heard the screen door whine its way open as Nick and Mandy slipped inside. Cyril had had a feeling they'd come back.

Like he hadn't done for two long years, Cyril responded to Nick's entrance with nothing more complicated than, "Hungry?"

And like Nick hadn't done for two long years, he grabbed the remote, kicked off his vintage orange sneakers, and flopped onto the oversize rust-colored couch that faced the kitchen TV. "Starving." Mandy curled up on top of his feet, asleep before her chin even dropped to her paw.

Cyril was happy with this conversation. Sure, they could talk about the past, about the forts they'd built in the woods long since toppled, grade-school high jinks since forgotten, high scores long since broken. They could talk about New York, about why he went and about why he came back. They could talk about Nick's mom, about rehab, about whether or not she'd ever be cured. Clearly Nick was back because he was old enough to take care of himself now, and he'd be doing just that. It was a big house and his mom was lonely in it, and they could probably be friendly, if little more. At least,

25

Cyril was pretty sure that was the deal. They could talk about the future, about how Cyril would soon enough be cooking at the AICA and Nick would be headed to college. They could talk about any of this stuff. But Cyril was happy to let their actions speak for themselves, and Nick was, too. That had always been their way.

Nick switched on the TV and flipped around a little before settling on some Jackie Chan flick.

Cyril pulled an apron over his head and began harvesting supplies from the fridge. Bacon, eggs, Tabasco sauce, ketchup, some onion he'd chopped a few days before while experimenting with empanadas. Cyril experimented a lot, so the fridge was always jammed with half-used ingredients—and Cyril *never* wasted anything. Real cooks never did.

He had laid a few strips of bacon into his favorite cast-iron pan, then turned on the flame underneath, when the phone rang. "Hello?"

"Hi, hon. Is your father there?" Cyril's mother was still on her nursing shift.

"Nope. But Nick is." Cyril liked the way that sounded.

"Nicky's there? He's in town? How is he? Did you feed him?" Mrs. Bartholomew asked with excitement in her voice. She, like Cyril, loved Nick.

"Working on it now. When are you getting home?"

"Not for a few more hours," answered Mrs. Bartholomew.

"I'll leave something out for you."

"I love you, Cyril. And send some food home with Nicky."

"Bye, Mom." Cyril hung up and inhaled. The smell of bacon draped the room.

"Mmm. Bacon," said Nick without looking up.

Cyril smiled. It felt so normal, so natural, to have Nick back on the couch, waiting for something to eat. Nick's mother had never bothered to use her state-of-the-art kitchen, so Nick had always eaten at Cyril's. Mrs. Bartholomew used to heat up lunch for the boys, but once Cyril had taken over in the kitchen, he'd become their primary maker of food. Cyril figured he'd cooked thousands of meals for Nick, some of them better than others, and he'd missed it. It felt good to be doing it again. Very good.

"So, Supermodel, what happened in New York?" Cyril grabbed a fork and started flipping the bacon strips one by one. He studied their color carefully, leaving one strip for a few extra seconds.

"Not much," Nick said, in typical style.

"Why'd you come back?"

"I got caught skipping school for two weeks straight."

"Dude, what were you thinking?"

"I don't know." Nick spoke absentmindedly, flipping channels the whole time. "I guess I was thinking it was time for me to get back to my buddy Cyril."

"Yeah, right. You never even called to say good-bye." Cyril was surprised he'd said it like that, just blurted it out. He hadn't been planning to. Part of him wanted to add, "I *needed* you around here," but he didn't.

"Called who?"

Cyril was surprised. "Called *me*!"

"I didn't?"

"No, you didn't." Cyril kept his eyes on the pan. "It would have been nice. I didn't know how to get in touch with you, you know."

"Sorry, man. I guess there was just a lot going on at the time. I guess I didn't want to drag anyone else into the whole thing. And then once I was in New York, I don't know, it just seemed like this place was so far away." Nick was still flipping channels. "Look! *America's Most Wanted*! I love this."

"Well, I was still here," mumbled Cyril to the bacon. But he decided to drop the subject, at least for now.

"Hey, Cyril?" Nick piped back up after *AMW* cut to a commercial.

"Yeah?"

"Does Rose have a boyfriend or anything like that?"

The question sliced through Cyril like one of his chef's knives, and he wanted to go back to the nonconversation. He didn't answer, just poked at the bacon and listened to its squeak-splatter for a moment. "Why?"

"I don't know. I was just wondering. She seems cool."

"Really? I would have thought you'd be into Jamie, not Rose," Cyril nudged.

"Well, don't get me wrong. Jamie's hot, but there's something about Rose. Something's going on behind those glasses." He flipped another channel. "She reminds me of this hippie chick I went out with in New York."

"Well, she's not," snapped Cyril.

"Not what?"

"Not the hippie chick you went out with in New York."

"I know that, dude. Take it easy."

Cyril laughed to defuse the moment. He swallowed, wishing the bacon would hurry up. He was really hungry and didn't like the taste in his mouth right now.

"She's definitely hippie-ish," Nick said. "In a hot way."

8 slices thick-cut streaky smoked bacon

1 small onion, cut into slices

6 large eggs, as fresh as possible

ketchup, salsa, Tabasco sauce, or other condiment
of your choice

1. Arrange slices of bacon in a large, *cold* cast-iron fry pan. (Starting them cold helps keep them flat.)
2. Place the pan over medium flame or medium-high heat and don't touch it for about 4 minutes. Carefully turn the bacon over with a fork or tongs and continue to cook 2–3 more minutes. Remove bacon; place carefully onto paper towels.
3. Return the pan to heat. Drop in the onions, and cook 8–10 minutes until brown and crispy but not burned.
4. Break the bacon into smaller pieces and return to the pan. Arrange it and the onions evenly around the bottom of the pan.
5. Crack the eggs into spaces between the bacon slices. Break the yolks or don't, depending on your mood. As eggs cook, everything will stick together.
6. After the eggs are almost cooked to your liking, cover the pan for 2 minutes.
7. There should now be a solid disk of eggs, bacon, and onions. Wrangle a spatula underneath; slide disk out of the pan onto a serving plate.

8. Slice like a pizza, douse with ketchup or hot sauce, and eat with your favorite toast. Or your favorite flavored Doritos.
9. Go to bed happy. (Sort of.)

Serves two hungry boys

cyril's soda bread

"Argh! I don't *know* if it works!" Cyril was pissed. "I've never *tried* it before! I'm just working from memory. The truth is I overheard the technique when I was washing dishes at the AICA!" He wanted to sound forceful, but he could tell it came out sounding panicked. "I'm out of baking powder. Where's the baking powder?" He looked intently at Alice. His khakis and sweatshirt were covered in flour.

"It's in the cupboard by your feet," said Alice Windemere, fiddling with the gray braid that hung off one tiny Polarfleece-covered shoulder. Alice was a small woman, short in stature but long in hair. "Listen, I've got customers, so shout if you need me, but only if you really need me." She ducked through the batik curtain and back into the store out front.

Cyril still wasn't used to Alice's kitchen. Ever since she'd opened Oregano in the Hudson Common strip mall a couple of years before, Cyril had been a constant fixture in her shop, sometimes spending hours talking with her about recipes or techniques, tasting her samples, even, recently, cooking with her . . . and hardly ever buying anything. Oregano was the only gourmet food store in the area, catering mostly to the AICA staff, and the prices were way too high for Cyril.

About a month ago Cyril and Alice got into a heated debate over the easiest way to draw juice from a chopped tomato. Cyril contended that it's not necessary to salt the tomato first, and Alice, who disagreed with him, invited him into her kitchen to demonstrate his point. He did and won the argument. He'd had total access ever since, and on Sundays like this one, when he wasn't working as an "assistant" in the student kitchens at the AICA, making $6.18 an hour, he was likely practicing for his upcoming AICA admissions audition, in Oregano's tiny galley kitchen with the stainless-steel countertops and frosted-glass windows. For the audition he would have to prepare three dishes in the AICA kitchens and then submit them to the admissions committee for approval. Cyril knew he had the talent, but the committee was notoriously unforgiving, even to gifted students. On audition day everything would have to be *perfect*. And this soda bread was anything but perfect. Instead of a soft-hard ball of dough, this was a lumpy, sticky disaster.

"I don't get it! It just keeps sticking to my hands. This recipe sucks!" Cyril knew he was talking pretty loud, but he didn't really care.

"Cyril?" Alice's voice was soft. She poked her bird body through the batik.

"What!" hurled Cyril, glaring at Alice but still prodding the sticky dough.

"You're yelling," she said. "Step away from the dough. Stop, have a glass of water, and figure it out."

Cyril knew she was right, but he didn't want to let go. He was pissed and wanted it to work *now*. He stared at his hands, covered with sticky dough.

Alice spoke again. "Cyril, listen to me. You're an incredible cook. Maybe the best I've ever seen. But you still have to be *present* when you're cooking. You can't phone it in, you know? Befriend your dough, don't fight it."

Cyril closed his eyes so Alice wouldn't see them roll. *Befriend my dough?* Was she kidding? He knew she'd lived in a commune for a while, but come *on*. He mulled it over for a bit. She might be nuts, but he also knew she was right. Fighting with this dough wasn't going to make it work. He'd have to work *with* it. Cyril stepped away from the dough and looked down at his One Stars. "Sorry. Didn't mean to blow like that."

"No problem, Cyril. I know the difference between kitchen talk and regular talk."

Cyril smiled at Alice and knew she was right. She'd spent something like thirty-five years cooking in some of the best (and worst) restaurants in and around the San Francisco Bay area. She knew everything about food, and he always listened when she spoke.

"Butter-and-sugar sandwiches, Cyril."

"Huh?"

"Great dishes have nothing to do with what you do to the food. They have everything to do with what you give to it. Being a great chef demands your heart, and not everyone knows how to give it. That's why one person's butter-and-sugar sandwich can taste like cardboard and another's can taste like heaven."

"Thanks," said Cyril, turning his back on the

dough. He'd had enough counterculture wisdom for one day. "Mind if I make us some tea?"

"Great idea. I'll take Lavender Wheel-o-Life." Alice looked at her reflection in the microwave. "By the way, dig my new hat! It's Afghani."

But Cyril, leaning back against the counter, was already nose deep in the latest edition of *Home Chef Illustrated*. "I can't believe there's another black-bean salsa in *HCI* this month. I hate black beans. They're so last century!"

He looked up to see Alice smirk. Encouraged, he raised a fist. "Unless I am in an open-air bazaar in Oaxaca, I declare that I'll never again swallow a black bean. Be it in a soup, a salsa, a quesadilla, or a fritter, keep it away. Bring me navy, cannellini, pinto, wax, green, or garbanzo beans, and I'll wave my fork with joy. But should a black bean appear on any plate of mine, I'll wave it like a sword. Let it be known, far and wide, that Cyril Bartholomew heretofore resolves to shun black beans forever." He paused for a beat, then muttered, "Unless of course they're on those fish tacos you make. I love those."

"Cyril, you're a trip."

Cyril loved when she said that. A sixty-year-old

saying *trip* was, well, a trip. He laughed, closed the magazine, and spun around. "I'm ready to befriend my dough."

"Cyril, hang on a second." Alice took over the tea-making process and lit the stove underneath the teapot. "Who are you making this bread for?"

"What do you mean?" asked Cyril.

"I mean, who are you making it for? You have to think of someone when you cook. That's the only way to make it good. You have to anticipate that look in their eye. You know the look I mean." Alice tore open a foil box of Swiss butter cookies. "Here, allow me to demonstrate." She raised the cookie to her mouth, and her eyes rolled back. "Mmm."

Cyril laughed. He knew the look well. It was the look of pure satisfaction. He'd even seen it on Alice's face once for real when he made her his famous tomato soup. "Yeah, I know the look. But this is just a practice loaf. I just want to see if I can do it."

"Trust me, Cyril. Have someone in mind. It'll change everything." Alice ducked back through the curtain.

Cyril went back to the loaf and, without trying to or even wanting to, conjured Rose. Her brown eyes half open, lashes casting a flutter shadow on her cheek as

37

she savored a fresh-from-the-oven warm piece of soda bread, crusty and golden on the outside, rich and soft on the inside, slathered with melted fresh-cream butter and warm wildflower honey, her lower lip glistening as she told him how she'd never tasted anything so delicious in her life.

Within moments Cyril's dough was at the perfect consistency. He was pretty sure that once it was baked, Alice would take one bite and get the famous-tomato-soup look. For real.

4 cups all-purpose flour

½ cup sugar

1 teaspoon fresh baking soda

1 tablespoon baking powder

½ teaspoon salt

1 tablespoon cinnamon (optional)

1 teaspoon fresh ground nutmeg (optional)

½ cup margarine, soft but not melted

1 egg

1 cup buttermilk

½ cup golden raisins

¼ cup (½ stick) butter, melted and cooled

1. Preheat oven to 375 degrees. Position oven rack in center spot. Grease up a large baking sheet using the paper the margarine came wrapped in.

2. Sift together the flour, sugar, baking soda, baking powder, salt, cinnamon, and nutmeg, if using. Sift two more times, three times total, ending in a large bowl.

3. Mix the margarine into the dry ingredients with a wooden spoon. Set aside.

4. In a small bowl mix together the egg and buttermilk with a fork. Add to the flour mixture and combine. Don't mix too hard. (If you over-work the dough, your bread will be really tough and chewy.)

5. Fold in the raisins. Gently.
6. Turn the dough out onto a cutting board that you've sprinkled with a little flour. Knead for exactly 1 minute. No more, no less. (See comment above about overworking the dough.) It should be loose, not sticky, and when you poke your finger into it, it should only spring back partway.
7. Form the dough into a round loaf. Carefully score a big X in the top with a sharp knife, being careful not to cut too deeply into the dough. (This will help the loaf bake into a big "flower.")
8. Brush the loaf with the melted butter. Bake for about 40 minutes or so, or until a toothpick inserted into the *middle* of the loaf comes out clean. Bread should be golden brown, crusty but not too hard.
9. Eat with plenty of butter.

Makes one large loaf

(Must be treated very gently. Measure all the ingredients very, very carefully. And follow all directions meticulously. Above all, befriend your dough.)

hot-buttered maple-baked oatmeal

The morning had begun perfectly, with Nick banging through Cyril's screen door at seven-fifteen, surprising no one. Without a word, he dropped his knapsack on the couch, then settled his boot-cut-jeaned self on a bar stool opposite where Cyril was cooking. "Hungry?" asked Cyril.

"Starving," came Nick's answer.

Cyril, in his favorite heather-gray sweatshirt, slid a steaming bowl across the counter to Nick, who plunged his spoon into the oatmeal as if he were four. It was just lumpy enough, creamy and soft, steaming with a fragrant maple steam. For the next several minutes the only noise that could be heard was the sound of spoons scraping against bowls and the occasional distant

Mandy bark from a far-off corner of Cyril's backyard. They finished quickly, and on the way out the door, when Nick stuffed a couple of the kitchen-sink cookies into his jacket pocket, Cyril handed him a small paper bag to carry them in instead.

"Thanks, Mom," said Nick.

"Ha-ha," retorted Cyril. "Very funny."

Everything was still going perfectly at ten thirty-two, when the entire biology class was vivisecting earthworms, but Cyril and Rose could *not* stop laughing.

"Bartholomew? Mulligan? Is your worm cracking jokes on your dissection tray? Does he moonlight as a stand-up comedian?" The shrill, tinny voice belonged to the legendary Mr. Meech, New Hyde Park Regional's most beloved, wackiest, and longest-serving teacher. Sometimes he was the funny Meech, and sometimes he was the mean Meech, and it was almost impossible to tell which Meech was in the building . . . often until it was too late. "Please, share this rare humor with us. This place is as boring as a biology lab." The Meech's hands tapped impatiently against his polyester-clad hips.

Cyril, betting that The Meech had his sense of humor on today, stepped up for a swing. Laying his hands on his stomach, he took the floor like a barrister. "Okay, Mr. Meech. What kind of coffee do earthworms like best?" He looked over at Christina Cartagena, the proverbial girl-in-the-front-row-of class, who was actually taking notes on this exchange.

Rose tugged on his sleeve. *"Sit down!"* she whispered.

"Yes, Bartholomew?" The Meech looked over his glasses. He appeared dangerously close to losing control of his comb-over.

"Fresh ground." Cyril poker-faced it, then looked down at Rose, who had collapsed in peals of laughter. This got Cyril beaming, loving nothing more in the world than making her laugh. Looking back at Christina, he winked. "This won't be on the test, Christie." She put her pen down.

"Thank you, Bartholomew. Now, get to work." The Meech grinned widely. Cyril sat down.

Cyril mimicked The Meech in a whisper. "Begin the vivisection, Mulligan."

Rose, tucking her hands into the sleeves of her knobby brown turtleneck sweater, whispered back, "I can't! It's alive! You know I can barely crush a mosquito! I won't even eat tuna from a can! Dead animals and I do *not* mix! You do it." Rose held out the scalpel. She turned her face away in mock horror.

Cyril smiled, agonized at how adorable she could be. "Aw. You are the original vegetarian, aren't you?" Cyril took the scalpel. He pressed against the blade with his thumb. Nice and sharp. This was nothing. Cyril had been spared the squeamish gene. He was used to dropping live, thrashing lobsters face first into boiling salted water. He could debone a chicken in six minutes flat. "Avert your gaze, milady."

Rose started giggling again. *"Milady?"*

"Mulligan? Is there a problem with the vivisection procedure?" The Meech was standing behind them, casting a bony, ancient shadow over their experiment.

"No—no," stammered Rose. "I just don't think I can . . ." She trailed off and looked over at Cyril, panicked. "Help!" she mouthed silently.

There was a snicker at the back of the room, unmistakably Brandon Keifler. *"I just don't think I can,"* he mocked to his buddies, who chuckled deferentially. This pissed Cyril off.

"Shut up, Brandon," Rose snapped.

Cyril came blazing to the rescue. "She has a point, Mr. Meech," he said. "She was just saying, couldn't we use one of the worms you sliced open for the demonstration? You did bisect several of them. That way we won't waste any. Surely we don't want to waste worms." Cyril looked at Rose and smiled, then back at The Meech. "Right?"

Silence. All eyes on The Meech. Christina Cartagena's pen had stopped dead. He strolled wordlessly back to his desk, science-teacher shoes squeaking on the linoleum, collected the dead worms, and returned to Cyril and Rose's tray. "Good point, Rose." He continued strolling through the room. "Back to work, everyone!" Christina went back to her note taking, and Cyril sat back down, flushed and smiling.

Rose leaned over, mouth to Cyril's ear, and whispered, "Thank you. You're amazing." He could feel her breath on his earlobe, and Cyril felt his face heat up even more. "I hate Brandon."

Cyril felt like he'd just won a joust. Now his fair lady would hop on the back of his horse and they'd ride out of the arena. He and Rose went on with the dissection, Cyril wielding the tools, Rose recording their findings. And then, out of the blue, Rose looked up at him and announced, "Nick's in my French class." And just like that, Cyril fell off his steed.

"Oh?" Cyril felt that taste rise up again in the back

of his throat, the taste of something he could have never come up with on his own.

"Yeah, he's way ahead of the rest of us. He must have had a good teacher in New York or something."

"Oh," was all Cyril could say, or mumble, to be more specific. His mind was so full of questions—had Nick flirted with Rose? Had Rose given Nick her number? Did she like him? Had they kissed? Did she like him? He had no brainpower left for forming words. He also didn't feel like bothering to say that if anybody had given Nick a good grounding in French, he had, two years earlier. Nope. He'd be better off keeping all that inside, where it'd be right at home with all the other things he couldn't say.

"Does he have a girlfriend?" asked Rose.

He tried to chalk her question up to generic interest. When someone new comes to school, boy *or* girl, it's only natural for the other students to wonder about him or her, right?

"I don't know," he answered, and for all he knew, Nick might well have a girlfriend. Cyril hoped that was the end of the questions.

And for a moment, it was.

Then Rose muttered, "I wonder if he can cook."

Cyril dropped his scalpel to the floor with a clang much too big for such a small object. "What do you mean?"

"I mean, if he can speak French, then he's into romantic things. And I love a guy who can cook. It's so . . . romantic." She sighed. "But whatever, who cares. It's not like I want a guy in my life, anyway. I guess it's just a thing I have." She looked up at Cyril, gently smiling. "Like when I thought you were baking those cookies the other day, it was kind of hot." Rose smiled, almost flirtatiously. But not quite. "Yes, my fantasy man, the one who I'll probably never meet in this town of Keiflers, will be an amazing cook."

This almost sounded like music to Cyril, only way off tune. Not to mention way more than he was prepared to take in all at once. "Uh, I think we should clean up now." He crouched down to get the scalpel.

He was on his knees, out of sight, when he heard the voice of Brandon Keifler, who was returning his dissection tray to the front. "How'd the dissection go, Rose? Did it make you hungry? I know how you *love* fresh meat."

"Shut up, Brandon."

"Speaking of fresh meat, looks like you're getting

along really well with Mr. Two Tons of Fun, Cyril. Why would a hot girl like you be slumming like that?" Brandon said, just under his breath.

"Now, why would you call him that?" asked Rose. Her tone was so sincere, Cyril wondered if maybe her glasses had a slimming effect. Like those mirrors at department stores that make people look thin so they'll buy things.

"Just leave me alone, Brandon. Cyril is my *friend*. But I wouldn't expect you to understand that."

My friend. It should have made Cyril feel good, but this particular reality check hit him like a punch.

"Just kidding, Rose. Take it easy."

"Shut up, Brandon." She said it again, and the third time was a charm. Cyril stayed crouched down, out of sight, until he was sure Brandon was gone. If he pretended he hadn't heard it, then maybe it hadn't happened.

The bell rang, and Cyril was saved. He stood up and began stuffing his books under his quickly dampening armpit.

"Thanks again for saving me back there, Cyril." Rose pulled her ponytail out from under her hat as students started to file out.

Cyril couldn't wait to get out of there. "I didn't do anything," was all he could muster.

Cyril followed Rose out into the hallway, hoping the din of New Hyde Park Regional's three thousand students, especially Christina Cartagena and her crew of smarty-pants chatterbugs, would drown out any chance of conversation. No luck. But Rose went on, anyway. "Seriously. I mean it. Most guys would have just thought I was being stupid about the worm. Brandon obviously did. But not you. Thanks."

"No, I didn't think you were being stupid," Cyril answered. "I think it's cool to have strong convictions."

"See what I mean?" Rose stopped, took Cyril's arm, and looked him square in the face. He shifted his gaze from her left eye to her right and back again. *Brown-eyed girl.* She lifted her other hand to his cheek, cupping it in her palm. "See what I mean?" she said again. Cyril wished she would say something else, something like, *I love you.* But then she said, "Someday, Cyril, some girl's going to be really lucky to have you. I wonder who she'll be?"

"Yeah, I wonder!" the voice came from behind Cyril. "I wonder who she'll be!" It was Nick, pushing his way through the crowd. "Hey, guys."

"Nick!" piped Rose.

Nick turned back to Rose. "How was biology?"

49

"How did you know I just came from biology?" asked Rose, grinning.

For all his girth, Cyril suddenly felt like the invisible boy.

"Lucky guess," answered Nick, then pointed to her chest, against which she was holding her *Living Biology* text. Nick wiggled his eyebrows.

Cyril felt like telling them both to get a room.

"Hey, do you know where the principal's office is? I need to get these forms signed."

"Dude, I just showed it to you yesterday," Cyril started. But Nick wasn't asking him.

If Nick had been anyone else, Cyril would have been pretty turned off by this paper-thin charade. But Nick wasn't anyone else. Nick was Nick. And he wasn't putting on a charade. He had genuinely forgotten where the principal's office was. And that he had ever asked Cyril about it in the first place. Nick was just being his lost self. He was like some clueless woodland creature, and Cyril couldn't think of anyone who liked animals and wanted to take care of them more than . . . Rose. "It's downstairs," said Rose. "Come on, I'll show you." She tugged at Nick's arm.

"Uh . . . you guys, I know where the principal's office is, too," said Cyril. "Great lab, Rose."

Great lab? Who says that? Cyril wished he could rewind and come up with something witty and creative. Not that it would have mattered. He wished that his gallantry in the lab counted for anything. But it didn't. Rose was with Nick now, way down the hallway.

2 cups old-fashioned oats (Don't use quick oats.)

pinch salt

⅓ cup maple syrup

3 cups whole milk

1 egg

1 tablespoon vanilla extract

¼ cup brown sugar

1 teaspoon cinnamon (optional)

raisins, coconut flakes, or almonds (optional)

1. Preheat oven to 350 degrees. Position rack in middle of oven.
2. In a large bowl combine oats and salt.
3. In a smaller bowl mix together the maple syrup, milk, egg, and vanilla. Pour over oats; mix well.
4. Pour the oat mixture into a glass baking dish. Bake for about 40 minutes, stirring once midway through. Remove from oven.
5. Sprinkle the oats with brown sugar and return to the oven for 5 minutes. The brown sugar will get all melty, which is exactly what you want.
6. Serve in warm bowls with a big hunk of butter and a drizzle of maple syrup that you've zapped in the microwave for about 30 seconds. Top with cinnamon, raisins, coconut flakes, or almonds, if desired.

Serves four

homemade fig cookie bar thingies

"Cyril, when can I expect to see your completed SUNY application?"

"Um . . ." Cyril said.

It was that defining day in September when the air was more cool than warm, and everything seemed to change from green to orange. But Cyril, who loved that day, was stuck in a mandatory meeting with Ms. Jackson, NHPR's college counselor. Ms. Jackson sat in her overstuffed chair, wearing her usual oversize cable-knit sweater with oversize silver-and-turquoise earrings. She was busily overwhelming Cyril with a barrage of unnecessary questions. Since Cyril had only one plan, the AICA, this meeting was an exercise in faking interest in the State University of New York just to make Ms. Jackson happy.

"When is the application due?" Cyril asked, and coughed politely into his hand.

"January."

"Um, how about January?"

"Cyril, SUNY is a very good option for you. You can't rely on the AICA. It's incredibly difficult to get accepted. In fact, no New Hyde Park student has made it into the AICA in over eight years. I doubt, very highly, that you'll get in."

Cyril had heard this before, so it was easy for him to tune out. Besides, he had other things to think about. Like the fact that Rose and Nick were, at that very moment, holing up together in the language lab, cramming for a French quiz together. What a laugh—Cyril couldn't believe that Nick had Rose convinced that he was good in French—Cyril was much better in French any day of the week. So much so that he'd probably be doing both Rose and Nick a favor if he took a stroll over to the language lab and checked in to see how things were going. Yes, that would be the perfect thing to do if MS. JACKSON WOULD EVER STOP TALKING AND LET HIM OUT OF THIS STUPID MEETING.

"Could we get on with this? I've really got to get going," Cyril said.

"Cyril! This is your future we're talking about. Let's take our time with it, shall we?"

"Oh," Cyril said. "Okay. Sorry."

"Now, where were we?"

Finally at four o'clock Ms. Jackson let Cyril out, but only after he promised her to join the Ornithological Society to beef up his extracurriculars. He had a half hour to get to the AICA for a four-thirty shift.

He passed through the empty NHPR halls, headed straight for the language lab at the far end of the ground floor. Bursting into the room, he was greeted by stares from two students he'd never seen before, both drowning in earphones. There was no sign of Rose or Nick anywhere. Cyril wasn't sure what that meant, but he was pretty sure he didn't like it.

Cyril ran out the lab door and headed for the south stairs, where everyone who had nothing better to do hung out after school. But no sign of Nick and Rose. He spun around and sprint-strode to the cafeteria. But the lunchroom was empty, too. Out of long habit he stopped breathing through his nose while he scanned the room. He crossed to the rear entrance, caught his breath, and made his way through to the gym. But the lights were out and the doors were bolted shut.

Cyril checked his watch again. Four-ten. Even at top speed, with no delays on the bus, he would only barely make it on time. He resigned himself to giving up the search. He was probably being crazy, anyway. Whatever urgency he was feeling about helping Rose with her French was obviously in his head. Besides, he *had* to get to work on time. He couldn't afford to piss off the AICA administration, especially since he was hoping to snag a couple of hours in the practice kitchen after his shift and get acquainted with the setup there for his audition. Shoulders slumped halfway, Cyril headed for the north doors, knowing he could shortcut from there across the soccer field and pick up Poughkeepsie Transit at the far end.

As he stepped down the first of the four steps that led down from the doors, he shrugged one shoulder to readjust his backpack. This disturbance to his balance caused him to lose his footing, and in a terrible and all too familiar moment, he slipped.

Once he was airborne, everything went into slow motion. He couldn't tell which way was down, so he threw up his hands to catch himself wherever he might land, sending his knapsack soaring. Even upside down, he could see it was unzipped. Then the brick and concrete of the school spun in front of him, giving way to the cement of the sidewalk. He hit the ground with the side of his face in a heavy splat that sent shock waves down to his One Stars.

Thanks to his extra padding, Cyril felt little pain. But the humiliation and panic came on like gangbusters. He needed to stand up, quickly, before anyone caught sight of him. He rolled onto his stomach and pushed himself up to his hands and knees. Breathing heavily, he reached for his knapsack but lost his balance and fell again to the ground.

"Dude!" A brassy voice came from directly above him.

He looked up, and there, hand outstretched, was Jamie, massive hair pulled up into a blue handkerchief, eyes covered by police sunglasses, wearing a Metal Bike Company baseball tee.

Cyril's thoughts immediately went to Rose and the look that would be on her face when Jamie described the sight of him, chubby cheek to the ground.

Rather than taking her hand, Cyril lunged to his feet, dusting off the side of his face.

"So I guess you saw." Jamie shook her head.

"Saw?" asked Cyril. Cyril couldn't imagine there was something besides his recent performance to see. He was sure he was the only game in town. "Saw what?"

"Exhibit A," said Jamie. And with a grand, game-show-hostess sweep of her right arm, she turned dramatically toward the parking lot.

There was Nick's old car, The Shadow, an old Oldsmobile that his grandfather had given him. On the hood of the Shadow, sitting so close that their silhouettes were one, were Rose and Nick. Cyril couldn't see their faces, but he could see Nick reaching into a paper bag and feeding Rose with whatever was inside. And she was feeding him back.

Cyril rubbed his eyes and shook his head. For all the hours he'd spent imagining this scene and many others like it, he was completely unprepared for the live version.

And while he couldn't bear to watch, he couldn't turn away, either. He needed to take it in. He also needed to identify what it was that they were feeding each other. By squinting, Cyril was able to see the food substance in question more clearly. It was none other than his original-recipe kitchen-sink cookie. When Cyril had stuffed a bunch of them in Nick's bag this morning, he hadn't known that they would end up in Rose's mouth, via Nick's fingers.

"I've been trying to fix her up with a decent guy ever since that jackass Brandon screwed her over, but would she go out with any of them? No-o-o . . . all she ever said was that she hates guys and that she never wants to date again as long as she lives. She even got me to agree to be her date to the homecoming dance because she was done with guys—that's why she needed to have that private conversation with me at your party, in case you were wondering. I'm thinking that maybe she asked me to go with her so Nick wouldn't be able to ask me. I mean he was definitely flirting with me that night, and now check it out! It's like a shrink-wrapped Abercrombie and Fitch catalog over there!" When Jamie finally came up for air, she paused and turned to Cyril, who was vaguely aware of her chattering. "Girls, huh? Freakin' crazy. I don't get 'em. Do you?"

Cyril was on sensory overload. He had no idea how to respond. "I—I—" he stammered.

Jamie turned to him. "You what?" she started to ask, but when she saw the look on his face, she froze. "Uh-oh. Cyril. Are you okay?"

He still didn't answer.

"Cyril, you're *green*. Are you sure you're okay?" asked Jamie.

Cyril wished she would just leave. He spun around, facing away from her and everyone else, and dropped to his knee, pretending to tie his shoe. He desperately wanted to be alone, and even though there was no one else anywhere near them, he felt crowded by Jamie.

Jamie bent over and picked up a crumpled paper bag. "Hey, you dropped this." She shook it, listening to the sound it made. "What is it?"

Cyril stood up. "Huh?"

"This!" She thrust the little paper bag into Cyril's hand. "It's yours. What is it?"

"Um, I'm not sure." He handed it back to her. "Is that mine? I don't know where it came from." Cyril smiled weakly. "It must be something from home, I guess." He was already late and humiliated, not to mention brokenhearted. The last thing he needed right now was a food-issue moment.

"Well," she said, undeterred, "let's have a look." She stuck her hand in the sack and came out with a crumbly, biscuit-y cookie with mashed . . . *something* . . . slathered over the top. "Can I have one?" she asked as she popped it in her mouth. "Cthyril, thith ith delithious!" she exclaimed, full mouthed and wide-eyed. She swallowed. "Yum!"

"You can have them," said Cyril, picking up a pen. He looked over to see Jamie flipping through Cyril's AICA catalog.

"Hey, is this yours?" Jamie asked, bending over some papers still lying on the sidewalk.

"Huh?" asked Cyril. He reached out his hand without looking up.

"Chef's school, huh?" she asked, reading the cover.

Cyril snapped the catalog, stuffed it away, and zipped up his backpack. "I must have grabbed it by accident at work. I work at the AICA, you know."

"Really. Cooking?"

"Uh, no. I just wash dishes. No big deal." Cyril was talking fast, mostly because he didn't want to be having this discussion. Or any other discussion, for that matter.

"Really," said Jamie. "That's a pretty long bus ride just to wash dishes." She was studying him intently.

"See you later, Jamie." He turned and took two steps away. He'd had it with questions for a while. The only good questions were the ones that had good answers, and lately, good answers seemed to be in short supply.

Filling:

1 cup sugar

1½ cups dried figs, chopped into tiny pieces

½ cup walnuts, also chopped into tiny pieces

½ cup water

Put all the ingredients into a medium pot. Place it over high heat until it boils, then reduce the heat to low and let it bubble away for about 10 minutes, stirring frequently. It should get all gooey and thick. Set it aside to cool.

Cookie Part:

1 cup brown sugar

1 stick unsalted butter, softened

pinch salt

1 teaspoon fresh ground nutmeg

2 teaspoons vanilla extract

2¼ cups all-purpose flour

2 cups old-fashioned oats

1. Preheat oven to 350 degrees.
2. Using an electric mixer on its highest setting, cream together the sugar and butter until it's all fluffy and light in color. This takes about 3–4 minutes.
3. Mix in the salt, nutmeg, and vanilla. Set mixer

to low, then stir in 1¾ cups of the flour and all the oats until it's all crumbly.

4. Pat two-thirds of the cookie mixture into an ungreased 9x13x2-inch pan.

5. Spread the cooled fig-and-sugar mixture evenly over the top.

6. Add the rest of the flour to the cookie mixture and crumble it all over the top.

7. Bake for 25–30 minutes. Allow to cool in pan, then cut into bars.

Makes about twenty-four bars

fried-onion soup

"She *loves* those kitchen-sink cookies. Can you believe it? She couldn't believe I'd made them."

And Cyril couldn't believe what he was hearing. He had stopped in at Wal-Mart on his way home from work to pick up some fried-onion soup fixin's. Nothing like a bowl of sautéed onions covered in a sheet of melted cheese to distract him from his troubles. Of course, any hope of distraction flew out the window as soon as he ran into Nick. What had the world come to if a guy couldn't shop at Wal-Mart in peace?

"Really? I wonder why!" Cyril was at full stride, racing down aisle seven. If only Rose had had one bite of a kitchen-sink cookie at the party. Then maybe she would have recognized the taste and realized she was being duped.

"Well, no. I mean, I didn't tell her I made them. But I didn't tell her I didn't make them, either. I just thought you wanted to keep the whole chef thing undercover. You're the Undercover Chef, bro!"

Cyril didn't answer. What could he say? Nick was right—no one was supposed to know about Cyril's cooking. Nick was the absolute and only friend Cyril trusted with that information. Nick didn't care about Cyril's weight. It was almost as if he didn't see it.

"Batman, seriously, what's up? It's not like you like her or anything, is it?" Nick had almost caught up with him.

What was the point? Cyril scoffed, walking faster. He didn't care. She obviously already liked Nick. They could do whatever they wanted. "She's not just another girl, you know. Rose is *special*."

"I know, man. No worries." Nick tried to high-five Cyril, but Cyril didn't feel like bonding now. So he pretended to be too immersed in the intricacies of comparative blowtorch shopping to notice. He was admiring a really expensive one when Nick interrupted the research. "Hey, dude. Can you teach me how to cook?"

Cyril didn't mask his shock. "What? You want to learn how to cook?"

"Yeah. You know, like you do. Can you give me a lesson?"

That hurt. As if it took just a lesson to learn to cook. He wasn't sure what to say. He struggled to sound uninterested. "Um, why do you want to learn how to cook?"

"I want to cook dinner for Rose."

"Uh, okay." Cyril kept moving.

"What? Don't you think she'd like that? I mean, she was really into those cookies yesterday. She was really impressed. So I was thinking, why not make her something really special?"

"Why don't you just ask her out like a normal person?"

"Because, Cyril. She must get asked out all the time. I want to do something different. I want to take care of her. I already tried asking her out for homecoming, but she and Jamie are going together. Cooking dinner for her seems like the next-best thing."

He wants to *take care* of her? Cyril choked, then caught his breath. "Why stop at dinner, man?" he tried to joke. "Why not cook her a surprise five-course gourmet meal? Why not just morph yourself into an Iron Chef?"

"Dude!" yelped Nick, clueless. "Now you're talking! Can you help me?"

"Can I help you?" he muttered under his breath, and tried to squeeze past the superstore clerk.

"Can I help you?" The name tag hanging from her polyester tunic said Arlene. She was twirling her price gun like a weapon. She was snapping her gum like the receptionist at the AICA, the one who was never, ever nice to Cyril.

"No, thanks," answered Cyril quickly. "Excuse me," he said as he skirted past, bumping into her.

"Yeah, excuse you," said Arlene. "Big and tall clothes are the other way," she sneered.

Cyril pretended he didn't hear and hoped Nick would do the same. He walked on. Nick stopped.

"Come on, Nick," said Cyril. "Let's go." He walked around behind Nick and pushed him along.

"No." Nick wriggled free. "Cyril, I think this young lady just said something to us, and I didn't hear her so clearly. I'm sorry, *Arlene*." Nick squinted at her name tag. "I didn't hear you. What did you say?"

"It's Ar-*lay*-na," said Arlene.

"My mistake, Ar-*lay*-na. Emphasis on the *lay*, correct? Nice smock you're wearing there. Would you mind repeating what you said?"

Arlene's gum-snapping slowed. She stared blankly

at Nick. Cyril noticed she had rings on every finger, including her thumbs. "Nothing," she muttered.

"I didn't think so," said Nick, glaring at her.

Nick turned back to Cyril, mouthing, "Let's go." Suddenly Cyril felt really bad about refusing to help him. Nick had a good heart and stood by Cyril's side, never worrying about what that did to his image. The least Cyril could do was return the favor.

"So, Supermodel, what should we make for your dinner with Rose?"

What did Cyril have to lose, anyway? It wasn't as if he ever had a chance with Rose himself. And besides, Cyril couldn't leave Nick alone in the kitchen—the idea of treating food that way made him too sad.

¼ stick butter

4 tablespoons olive oil

3 large yellow onions, sliced into rings

2 cloves garlic, finely chopped

2 tablespoons flour

dried herbs of your choice, such as thyme, tarragon,
    or savory (sniff the jars to figure out what you like)

kosher salt and fresh pepper to taste

8–10 cups chicken, vegetable, or beef stock

French bread

¾ cup grated Swiss cheese, such as Gruyère

1 can Durkee fried onions (optional)

1. In a cast-iron frying pan over high heat, heat up half the butter and half the olive oil until bubbling.
2. Before butter turns brown, throw in one sliced onion and fry over high heat until crispy and slightly blackened, about 10 minutes. Set aside and don't eat. At least, not all of it.
3. In a soup pot over medium-high heat, melt the remaining butter and olive oil. (You might need a little extra olive oil here.) Before butter turns brown, throw in the remaining onions. Cook slowly, stirring constantly with a wooden spoon, until onions become a rich brown color and the smell starts to make you salivate,

about 15–25 minutes. Remove the pot from heat, toss in the garlic, and stir well.

4. Return the pan to heat. Add the flour, and stir well. Add the herbs, salt, and pepper; stir well. Slowly pour in the stock and bring to a low boil. Simmer for at least 30 minutes, allowing flavors to blend together. While soup is simmering, heat up the broiler for cheese.

5. Slice the French bread into rounds and toast lightly. Arrange toasted rounds on a cookie sheet and sprinkle with grated Swiss cheese. Slide under the preheated broiler until the cheese is melted and just starting to turn brown and bubbly, about 2 minutes. (Keep your eye on it because it'll burn if you're not careful.)

6. Place the toasted bread with cheese into bowls. Ladle the soup over the top of the bread. Cover the top with crispy onions. Sprinkle with Durkee fried onions as well, if desired. Serve with a green salad.

Makes four bowls

two-fondue feast

*S*omehow, somewhere between feeling like he owed Nick one and believing that this was as close as he'd probably ever get to Rose, Cyril had agreed to mastermind an elaborate, romantic surprise for Rose. One that he knew she'd love, because he knew her well. Besides, it's not as if he had anything else planned for homecoming night.

First there was the shopping. Nick dipped into the "maintenance fund" set up by his father before he and Nick's mom had split up. Cyril hit the Hyde Park Farmer's Market, Coleman's Dairy, and Oregano. Nick set out to Poughkeepsie Cheese Bros. for a pound of Swiss Gruyère.

"Should I get anything else while I'm there?" Nick had asked. "Some steaks or something?"

"Nick. Gorgeous isn't everything. Now, pay attention: Your alleged prospective and as-yet-unattained date is a vegetarian." Cyril had looked over at Nick, who appeared stunned. "It's spelled *v-e-g-e*—"

"She is? I mean, uh, I knew that."

Cyril managed to get the shopping done before his three o'clock shift at the AICA and was back at Nick's colossal, chilly, empty house by seven-thirty. He fumbled through the poorly laid out kitchen and pressed his hands flat on the white marble countertops. He couldn't find a cutting board. He couldn't find a knife. He was glad he'd brought his own supplies.

Nick got the simple but time-consuming job of washing, drying, and recrisping the lettuce. Cyril attacked everything else.

While Cyril put the meal together, he couldn't help thinking of Rose. Her face floated in front of him as he sliced shallots. He pictured the curve of her jawline just below her ear as he shaped potatoes. He imagined her ponytail caressing the back of her neck as he chopped a chiffonade of herbs. He wondered what she'd say, what she'd do, when she tasted this meal. And then he tried not to think about it.

Cyril worked with focus and efficiency. Knives

flew, cupboards closed and opened, flames were lit, ingredients prepped, shaped, seasoned, and stacked. Cyril navigated the kitchen like an athlete, moving from sink to island to stove top. Seamlessly and swiftly the bags of groceries were transformed into neat piles of ingredients.

"Dude. You are seriously in the zone!" teased Nick. The zone was their name for the state that overtook Cyril when he got into a cooking groove. Cyril didn't respond, focused instead on peeling garlic cloves.

When Nick went upstairs to change, Cyril did a progress check. The bread was toasted and torn. The cheese was grated and piled high. The potatoes were roasting, filling the room with their aroma. The vinaigrette was whisked, the half-and-half was measured, and the chocolate was shaved. Cyril walked through the house and out the back door to the Spanish-tiled patio, where he had set the table on this mild, Indian-summer evening. Two copper chargers were down, and several candles were set, ready to be lit. The blackened steel silverware was laid carefully; salt and pepper shakers stood at the ready. There was a pyramid of pears and apples in the corner. The table was well arranged, but it seemed lifeless to Cyril. He scratched his head.

Suddenly Nick burst onto the patio, smoothing his hair. "How do I look?"

Cyril turned to him. *What do you expect her to say when she finds out the truth?* Cyril wasn't sure for a moment whether he'd really said it or not. He hoped not. He was determined not to let his feelings for Rose get in the way of this dinner.

"How do I look?" repeated Nick.

"Dude, you look great." Cyril said it before he'd even looked up. "Now, are you ready for Operation Rose Picker?"

After a frenzied final run-through and last minute wristwatch synchronization, Nick was out the door and behind the wheel of the Shadow. The plan was under way, and there was no turning back now. For better or for worse.

Nick couldn't have made it to the end of Shingle Camp Hill Road before Cyril's cell phone rang.

It was Nick, sounding anything but calm. "Shouldn't I bring her flowers or something?"

"Stick to the plan," Cyril said, and hung up. He walked back into the kitchen, where he began pouring the vinaigrette for the salad into a cruet.

Ten minutes later the phone rang again. "Dude! I'm in. I took the north doors, but it was close. There's, like, an army of girls in tube dresses and name tags here. I can barely move."

"Stay low," said Cyril, and hung up. He walked out to the patio, where he began positioning and repositioning the dozen or so candles he'd laid around the table. He knocked over the pear pyramid twice.

The phone rang again. Cyril answered it and said, "Get to the gym ASAP. Blend in and complete the mission quickly." He hung up and turned on Nick's over-the-top stereo. He slipped in a mellow trip-hop CD that Nick had burned the night before just for this evening.

Another ring. This time Cyril shouted, "What?"

The line sounded open, but there was no response. Cyril listened intently. He could hear the distant beats of Missy Elliot, a low rumble of voices punctuated by the occasional high-pitched squeal that only teen girls with too much adrenaline are capable of making, and the clack of high-heeled shoes on the lacquered gym floor. Cyril figured Nick, phone probably stuffed in his pocket, had accidentally hit redial.

"Aloha!" chirped a searingly high-pitched voice. "You've been lei'd! Ha-ha-ha-ha!" Cyril pegged the laugh as Christina Cartagena, homecoming committee chair, who was a little too psyched about the Moonlight at Waikiki theme she'd been talking about since home-coming last year.

Cyril continued to listen. The homecoming DJ had switched to a slow tune, and the voices quieted down a bit. Cyril heard Nick's sneakers squeak against the gym floor. Mandy panted her way into the kitchen, and Cyril tossed her a Milk-Bone.

"A moment like thiiiiiiis . . . !" The song wailed on, and even though he hated this sappy music, Cyril lost himself for a moment, wishing he were at the dance, holding Rose, swaying to the sap and declaring it *their* song. She would be a little taller in her heels. She'd be in black or green, and her hair would hang free around her shoulders. Behind her glasses her eyes would sparkle, and she'd breathe deeply next to him, nesting her head in his shoulder and kissing him lightly on the neck.

Cyril nicked his finger with the paring knife and dropped it. "Ouch." Fantasy moment over.

Cyril tuned back into the phone. He picked up more of Nick's wanderings, hearing random bits of conversation. And then pay dirt.

"Rose. Psst! Rose!" Nick was half whispering, half shouting.

"Nick!" whisper-shouted Rose. "What are you doing here?"

Nick cleared his throat. "You look unbelievable," he said. Pausing for a moment, he continued stiffly, "I've come to spirit you away. I've come to kidnap you to a better place. Come away." Cyril rolled his eyes. Nick was no actor. Cyril dropped the apple slices in a bowl of water with a spritz of lemon to keep them from going brown.

"No way! Jamie will kill me!" Rose protested. "What exactly do you mean, kidnap me?"

"I mean, kidnap you. I mean, take you away from here. I mean, a truly romantic evening. That's what I mean. Are you hungry?"

"I, uh . . . You look great, Nick. I want to go, I just . . . I already have a date. You know that."

"Jamie looks pretty busy over there with Trent Dufresne and Kyle Abrams." Cyril could picture Nick pointing across the dance floor toward Jamie, who was likely sandwiched.

"Be nice! She's my date!"

"Doesn't really look like it from here. Come on, Rose. What do you say?" Nick was probably down on one knee at this point. "Be my date instead and come away. I promise it'll be worth it."

"I, uh . . ." Cyril could hear her face crack into a smile. "These shoes are killing me."

There was a moment, a silent one. Cyril felt himself leaning in, listening intently. Were they kissing? Nick broke the silence, low and quiet. "Want a piggyback?"

"Yes!" Rose's shout was loud enough to sting Cyril's ear, and he jumped back. The muffled tussle of a piggyback leap and a small crash. "My glasses!" Rose shouted. "My glasses!"

Another muffled tussle was about all Cyril could take. He hung up the phone.

Cyril took a last pass around the patio to make sure everything was ready. He turned out the lights, then struck a match and lit the candles. The table and the patio, lifeless just a few minutes ago, warmed up in the vital, flickering glow. The glasses sparkled, the plates shone, the apples blushed. It all became beautiful.

When Nick's headlights appeared at the end of the drive, Cyril slipped back inside and turned the music up a notch. The music would give him extra cover. And besides, he didn't want to have to listen to them.

But by the time Nick and Rose stepped up onto the patio, Cyril knew the music wouldn't mask much of anything. He could hear plenty. "Oh, wow," Rose gasped and screamed all at once. Cyril guessed she'd just seen the candlelit table. "Wow! Nick! I . . . I don't know what to . . . what to say . . . !" Then silence for a moment. Were they kissing? "This is incredible."

"I'm glad you like it," said Nick. "Sit down. Say 'hey' to Mandy. I'll get us something to drink."

"Hurry back," said Rose.

Cyril heard the sliding door open, then close. Nick came sprinting into the kitchen to give a fist pump. "Yes!" he mouthed. "Sweet! This rules!"

Cyril could think of only one thing that would get Nick that excited. "Did you kiss her?" The question just slipped out before he had time to review the merits of playing it cool.

"Not yet, my man. Not yet."

Cyril rolled his eyes, handing Nick two spicy ginger sodas, and sent him back out to the patio. The words *not yet* implied *but soon*. Cyril thought this whole plan was starting to suck.

Cyril strained to hear Nick's toast. "Let them have their Moonlight at Waikiki! Here's to Moonlight at . . . um . . . Unnamed Upstate Location!" Their glasses clinked. Cyril shook his head as he gave the melted Gruyère a final stir, then poured the silky, bubbling fondue into Nick's family's brick-red, vintage 1970s fondue pot. He stuck a finger in the fondue and tasted. Perfect. He tossed on a few toast crumbs for a garnish, admired his work, and wondered if *not yet* was turning into *now*.

More sneakered footsteps down the hallway and Nick collapsed back into the kitchen. "Moonlight at Unnamed Upstate Location?" scoffed Cyril.

"I know, I know. It's all I could think of," Nick whispered, wiping his brow. "How are we doing in here, my captain?"

"I'm zoning," lied Cyril. "The fondue is ready. Get the bread and the fondue forks on the tray and I'll transfer the fondue now. Move."

Nick put the forks on the tray. Cyril was right behind him, setting down the fondue pot, now brimming with savory melted cheese. Nick picked up the tray, ready to head out back. "Wait!" Cyril barked. "The potatoes." He scraped a cookie sheet's worth of crispy potato wedges into a massive mixing bowl, threw coarse salt and pepper and herbs over the top, and tossed them around with a set of tongs. He poured them out onto a brick-red ceramic platter. They glistened.

Nick popped one into his mouth. "Ai!" he squealed.

"They're hot," said Cyril.

"Gee, thanks." Nick grinned. "Got any ketchup?"

Cyril scowled. "Uh, *no*. Get out."

"When do I come back?"

"After the fondue is gone, dumb-ass."

And Nick was back down the hall, back out the sliding door. Cyril listened for, and heard again, Rose's half gasp, half scream. "Wow! Nick, you're amazing!"

The next fifteen minutes were a blur of giggles, which were painful, and silences, which were torturous. Cyril lost himself in the sounds, in the nonsounds, and in the fantasy of Rose's brown eyes closing and opening with each bite.

"Where is it?" Rose's voice was shockingly close, and Cyril's eyes snapped open when he heard it. He took in his breath and held it. She was obviously inside the house.

"Um, it's upstairs." Nick, also inside, sounded nervous. There were footsteps in all directions.

"There's no bathroom down here?" The footsteps were closer now, just outside the kitchen door, and Mandy started to bark out on the patio. "What about through the kitchen?" Cyril, wide-eyed and still breathless, ducked behind the island, praying she couldn't see his shadow.

"No, no bathrooms down here!" Nick said. Cyril hoped Nick was thinking on his feet for a change. "Well, there is, but the, um, the toilet's broken. Yeah. The toilet. Trust me, you don't wanna go in there."

"Ah, gotcha," said Rose. The footsteps subsided and Cyril clamored to take back his breath. Straining, he could hear giggles from the back stairs.

Okay, now they're kissing.

After Cyril sent Nick out with the final course, the chocolate fondue, he crept down the hall to sneak a look through the sliding doors. He just wanted a quick look. He just wanted to see *her*.

When he got there, his breath went missing yet again. The patio, which had been lifeless and then beautiful, was now truly alive and exquisite. Rose was reclining on the bench in a rich brown crocheted halter dress, the same color as her eyes. Her legs were tucked underneath her skirt, brown sandals on the floor, kicked off who knew how long ago. Her chestnut hair fell around her shoulders, setting off her clear skin and making it seem even clearer. Mandy's sleeping head was in her lap.

Rose shivered, then reached behind her back and pulled a vintage shawl around her shoulders. Cyril ached to give her his jacket, or cup her hands in his, or turn off the breeze—anything to keep her from suffering a chill at that moment. But he stayed silent and invisible. Rose smiled at Nick.

Nick speared a strawberry onto a fondue fork and dragged it slowly through the satiny pot of chocolate that was several shades darker than her dress. He held it up to her mouth, which she opened, slowly, still smiling. She didn't close her eyes. She bowed her head to take the bite off the fork, but at the last second Nick pulled back the fork and replaced it with his face. "Hi, Rose," he said.

She stared at him a moment, startled. Then she breathed, "Hi."

Nick leaned in farther.

"You know," said Rose. "You should never get in the way of a girl and her chocolate."

Nick was the startled one this time. "What?"

"Chocolate," whispered Rose. She grabbed his wrist and brought the strawberry to her mouth. "Mmm," she said, closing her mouth around it.

Nick speared another strawberry, dipped it, and stuffed it in his own mouth. "Mmm," he mimicked her. Cyril wished he could stop watching.

She hit him playfully on the shoulder, and they both

laughed quietly, nervously. He leaned back in, next to her face. "Hi again."

And then came the moment Cyril had been dreading since the first time he saw Nick and Rose seated on the Shadow. Nick looked deeply into Rose's eyes, smoothed her hair back with his left hand, lifted her chin with his right forefinger, and kissed her. Once, quickly. Then again, slowly.

Even through the one-way glass Cyril could see their gazes lock as their heads pulled apart, and everything underneath his skin, from his brains to his blood to his bones, suddenly sank to his ankles. He struggled to move his feet, to get away from what he was seeing, but they were cemented. He tried to turn his head, but his neck was locked. He tried to close his eyes but couldn't will his lids. He was frozen, unable to stop watching as the girl he loved pulled his best friend in for another kiss.

"You taste like chocolate," Cyril heard her say.

Unworried about the noise he might make, Cyril walked solidly down the hall and out the front door, then turned left to walk up Shingle Camp Hill Road to home. He couldn't remember if he'd turned off the oven, but he wasn't sure he cared.

Cheese Fondue

1 clove garlic

1 loaf French baguette

1½ cups dry white wine (Almost all the alcohol burns off, so don't get all psyched.)

4 cups grated Gruyère cheese

½ teaspoon ground nutmeg

salt and pepper to taste

1. Slice the garlic clove in half. Rub the clove all over the inside of the fondue pot. (Wash your hands and rub a little lemon juice on them after this step or you'll smell like garlic for the rest of the night.)
2. Slice the bread into rounds. Toast the rounds, then tear into bite-sized pieces. Set aside.
3. In a large saucepan over high heat, bring the wine to a boil. Turn down heat to medium.
4. One handful at a time, toss the cheese into the wine, stirring as you add. When one handful melts, add another. Continue until all the cheese is added and the consistency is nice and smooth. Add the nutmeg, salt, and pepper.
5. Heat up the fondue pot. (Follow the instructions that come with the fondue pot.)
6. Pour the cheese into the fondue pot. Serve with torn bread and crispy potatoes.

(More than a bowl of melted cheese. It's a state of mind.)

Crispy Potatoes

4 medium potatoes, Yukon gold or red
1 tablespoon olive oil
1 tablespoon butter
coarse salt (sea salt or kosher salt) to taste
½ tablespoon chopped Italian parsley
fresh ground black pepper to taste

1. Preheat oven to 375 degrees.
2. Slice each potato into about six rounds, ½ inch thick. Pat with a paper towel until completely dry.
3. In a large oven-safe skillet (preferably cast-iron), over high heat, heat up the oil and butter until bubbling.
4. Using tongs, transfer the potatoes, one at a time, into the skillet. Watch out for spattering. Spread them out evenly in one layer. Don't crowd them.
5. Cook until crispy on the underside, about 5 or 6 minutes. Flip potatoes over. Cook on other side until crispy and brown. Sprinkle the potatoes with salt.
6. Transfer the skillet to the oven; bake about 15–20 minutes until nicely browned.
7. Remove from oven, and toss the potatoes in a large bowl with parsley, salt, and pepper.

A Simple Salad

2 big handfuls mixed greens
⅓ cup extra-virgin olive oil
2 tablespoons fresh lemon juice
1 tablespoon coarse Dijon mustard to taste (optional)
salt and pepper to taste

1. Thoroughly wash and dry greens.
2. If you have time, stick the greens back in the
   fridge for a couple of hours before you serve
   them. This will ensure that they're crispy.
3. In a clean jar with a top, pour the oil, lemon juice,
   and mustard. Close tightly, and shake well.
4. Add a pinch of salt and grind in some pepper.
   Shake again.
5. Toss the salad gently with a little of the dressing. Do *not* overdress the salad. Use less dressing than you think you'll need and add more
   only if needed.

Chocolate Fondue

½ cup half-and-half
1 12-ounce bar of good-quality chocolate (Dark chocolate is traditional, but pick your favorite, as long as it's good quality.)
2 teaspoons instant coffee powder
powdered sugar to taste (optional)
sliced bananas
strawberries
Sara Lee pound cake, cut up into cubes

1. In a small pan, warm up the half-and-half over low heat.
2. Break up the chocolate into chunks. Add chunks, one or two at a time, into the half-and-half. Stir after each addition, melting each chunk.
3. After chocolate is thoroughly incorporated, with no lumps, add the instant coffee. Turn off heat and stir slowly for 1 minute. Adjust sweetness with the powdered sugar if necessary.
4. Transfer the chocolate to a warm fondue pot. (If you're using the same pot as the cheese fondue, wash and rinse thoroughly first.)
5. Sprinkle the fruit with sugar, if desired, then spear fruit and cake, dip into chocolate, and let your eyes roll back in your head.

Dinner serves two

mustard grilled-cheese sandwiches

"*B*am!"

Cyril couldn't quite believe he'd actually sat through forty-five minutes of *Emeril Live*. The only good thing about it, as far as he could see, was that it was almost over. He reached for another grilled cheese, but the plate was empty. He got off the kitchen couch and skulked over to the counter to make more.

"Why do we add essence? *Because it makes it taste good!*" came Emeril's too loud delivery. The studio audience was cheering him through the pork chops he was smothering, responding like a congregation to a preacher. "Bam! *Woo-hoo!*"

Cyril hated *Emeril Live*. But he hated it in that way

that people hate *The Real World*. He hated it, but he loved to watch it.

"Shut *up!*" Cyril hissed at the TV as he spread mustard on a slice of toasted baguette. "You suck. And your studio audience sucks even harder! You wouldn't know a *mirepoix* from the Mir space station!" He layered on two slices of cheddar and four slices of Swiss. "You suck, blow, and everything in between!" Cyril slid the sandwiches under the broiler and watched them bubble. "Emeril sucks," he whispered to the grilled cheese.

He knew he was being a little psycho at the moment, but he also didn't care. He carried the plate of freshly grilled sandwiches back to his spot on the couch.

He wished he could explain this whole thing to Alice. He knew exactly what she'd say. Something like, *Cyril! Get a grip! No more! Focus on your own life. Let other people deal with theirs. Whether Rose and Nick end up loving each other or hating each other, you don't want to be in the middle.* She'd say it clearly like that; she'd make it make sense. That's what she did.

He just didn't really want to talk about it, though. With her or anyone. Cyril raised his third grilled cheese to his mouth. Or was it his fourth? He lay down on the couch to eat it.

It wasn't until he woke up that he even knew he'd fallen asleep on the couch. He was vaguely aware of Emeril, still *bam*-ing away, when he heard Nick's loud whisper outside the screen door.

"Mandy! Shhh! Sit. Lie down. Sit. Come on. Good girl. Okay, stay. Mandy, be good. I love you. I love you. Yes, I do."

Without opening his eyes, Cyril rolled them. He turned himself over on the couch, facing away from the TV. He tried to fall back asleep, knowing that sleep was his best defense against having to sit through all the details from Nick.

But still, there was something about Nick's arrival that made Cyril feel good. And besides, if Nick was with Cyril, that meant he wasn't with Rose, and that was a relief. Not quite as good as having Rose over and not Nick, but almost.

Cyril listened closely to the creaks in his house. He heard the screen door whine its way open and one floorboard after another give way under Nick's feet. He heard the groan of the refrigerator door and the squeak of Nick's sneakers against the wood.

And he heard Nick. "Cyril?" he whispered loudly. "You awake? Dude. We did it! Sweet! That chocolate was the clincher, dude. We pulled it off!"

Cyril, now entirely awake, kept his eyes closed and his breathing heavy and slow. He wanted Nick to stay quiet.

He felt Nick sit at the end of the same couch Cyril was stretched out on. *Clunk.* One sneaker kicked off. *Clunk.* The other. He heard Nick pick something up off the table, then listened as the channels changed from Food Network, to the *Twilight Zone* theme song, to the pitchman for Oxy-Clean, to a droning voice talking about the Three Gorges, to a rerun of *Scooby-Doo.*

Cyril heard Nick grab a grilled cheese, lean back, and crunch into it. Mandy's claws clicked along the floor before she heaved herself up on the couch with the boys.

"Mmm." Cyril felt Nick lean back on the couch. Then his voice. "We did it, man. Thank you. Thank you. Thank you."

Cyril listened as Nick finished his sandwich, then heard Nick crawl down onto the floor with one of the couch cushions. Maybe Cyril didn't want to hear all the sordid details of Nick's evening, but he couldn't overlook the fact that Nick had a queen-sized bed and a flat-screen TV with satellite just a few minutes' walk through the woods, yet he chose to sleep on the hardwood kitchen floor at Cyril's house that night.

The screen door squeaked open again, and for a moment Cyril wondered if Rose could be here, looking for him. Looking for Nick?

A voice said, "Hi, Nick." It was Cyril's mom.

"Hey there," Nick said. "Cyril's asleep."

"What did you do tonight?" she asked.

"Cyril helped me prepare this incredible dinner for an amazing girl. It was awesome, really."

"Oh, that's nice," she said. "Hey, Nick, I'm thinking of getting a Segway. Whaddya think of that?"

Is she seriously asking him that?

"I think you'd look great rocking a Segway, Mrs. Bartholomew."

He did not just answer her.

Between this absurd two A.M. conversation about scooters and cooking a romantic dinner for Nick and Rose, Cyril wondered if he had at some point stepped into a different dimension. But he was grateful, for once, that his mom wasn't overly interested in hearing all the gnarly details of his life.

1 loaf Italian sesame baguette

butter

country-style Dijon mustard

fresh basil

1 jar marinated sun-dried tomatoes (optional)

1 6-ounce hunk of cheese (cheddar, jack, Swiss, Gouda, whatever), shaved into thin slices

1. Preheat the broiler. Position oven rack in top slot.
2. Slice the baguette diagonally into large pieces. Brush the bread with butter, and toast lightly.
3. Spread toasted slices with plenty of mustard.
4. Lay basil leaves over the mustard.
5. Lay sun-dried tomatoes over the basil leaves, if using.
6. Layer cheese slices over the tomatoes.
7. Arrange the toasts on a cookie sheet, slide under the broiler, and toast until cheese turns gooey and bubbly and just begins to brown.
8. Eat open-faced.

Makes four sandwiches

(Better than any stupid old cheese fondue, anyway.)

pepitas (baked pumpkin seeds with cumin)

"Ew."

Cyril heard the *ew* from the girl standing behind him, scanning the fashion magazine section, but he didn't even look up to see who it was. He was hiding behind the latest issue of *Cucina Italiana*. He popped another buttery, crunchy, spicy pepita in his mouth, dribbling crumbs on the floor. The best part about the magazine section of Barnes & Noble was that you could have a snack while you browsed and no one got in your face about it.

"Ew!" She said it again. "Do you mind? God!" she scoffed.

Cyril looked up. He knew that hair. "Jamie?"

She spun around. "Cyril! You just got crumbs on my

toes!" Jamie kicked off her Dr. Scholl and wiggled her bloodred pedicure to dislodge a crumb.

"Sorry, sorry." Cyril, horrified, tried to play it cool.

"Gross!" gagged Jamie. She looked up, raised a tweezered eyebrow, and pointed at the bag. "Another mysterious bag of treats, Cyril? So what is it this time?"

"Uh, um . . ." He looked down for his One Stars, but all he saw were the black rubber shoes that were part of the AICA dress code. "I think they're called pepitas. They're toasted pumpkin seeds with salt. You want?" He held out a crumpled yellow paper bag.

"Uh, yeah! Duh!" Jamie quickly pulled up the sleeve of her denim jacket, stuck out her palm, and pointed at it impatiently. "Right here, killer. Hit me." Cyril poured out a few of the crispy little brown-orange seeds, and Jamie dumped the whole handful in her mouth. Her nostrils flared. "Mmm! Yum!" She kept chewing. "Cyril, where did you get these?" Instead of answering, he filled up her palm with another stream of salt and seeds. She crunched, moaning. "Mmm!"

Cyril crumpled up the bag and stuffed it in his backpack, dropping his magazine.

"What are you reading?" asked Jamie as she bent down to pick it up. "*Cucina Italiana*! Well, exsqueeze me!"

96

"Uh, I was just flipping through," said Cyril, quickly taking the magazine and sticking it back on the rack. "Killing time before my shift."

"You wash dishes, right?"

"Yeah."

"Well, that would explain the shoes," said Jamie. "Do you make good money? I need a job."

"No, you don't really work there to make money," said Cyril. He immediately wished he'd stopped at *no*.

"Then why work there?"

Cyril shrugged. "It's a job, I guess."

Jamie didn't say anything for a moment, but Cyril felt her eyes on him. He inhaled sharply.

"Well, I guess I'd better go," he said.

"Wait," said Jamie. "I'll give you a lift."

Cyril's attempt at a "No, thanks" was unsuccessful, and before he knew it, he was riding shotgun in Jamie's blue Nissan pickup, pouring another pile of pepitas into Jamie's hand. "These are so good!" she yelled above the radio. Cyril rolled down his window and stuck his head into the oncoming breeze. He loved doing that—it made him feel as happy as a dog.

Cyril pulled his head back in just as Jamie made a wide

left turn onto Route 43. As her Dr. Scholl went from pedal to pedal, she held out her hand for more pepitas. She steadied the wheel with her knee while reaching over with her nonpepita hand to shift. But the turn was wider than it should have been, and as she tried to correct it, her driving hand slipped off the wheel. Panicked, she accidentally hit the brake and her handful of seeds went flying.

"Damn!" she muttered, feeling for the accelerator and reaching wildly for seeds.

Jamie began to swerve, and Cyril realized he was the only one watching the road. "Jamie! Look out!" Cyril grabbed the wheel, and Jamie popped her head back up just as the passenger-side tire slipped off the shoulder of the road.

"Aaaaah!" she screamed. She slammed her foot against the brake and spun the steering wheel back toward the road. "Hold on!" Cyril looked down just as her Dr. Scholl slipped off the brake pedal, jerking the steering wheel out of her hand and sending the truck into a 180, spinning to a full stop on the far side of the road. The truck stalled. Cyril and Jamie bounced around, then settled.

They both stared straight ahead, silent. Even the radio had stopped.

"Rock and *roll*! Are we alive?" asked Jamie. She started cackling hysterically.

"I think so," said Cyril, following her into nervous laughter.

"High five!" squealed Jamie. They did. But Cyril could tell that Jamie had been scared out of her mind. Cyril certainly had been.

Before Jamie could start the truck back up, there was a knock at the back window. Jamie and Cyril turned around in unison, slowly. It was Nick, pressing his nose against the glass. "It's okay, I'm okay!" yelled Nick. "You didn't hit me! You came close, but you missed." He walked over to Jamie's side of the truck and looked over her at Cyril. "Hey, Cyril!"

"Hey, Nick," Cyril answered.

"Nick, I didn't see you!" Jamie gasped, rolling down her window. She began to laugh.

"Well," said Nick. "I guess that means you weren't trying to hit me on purpose."

"No," said Jamie. "If I wanted to hit you, I'd hit you."

"Oh yeah?" asked Nick. He was smiling wide.

Cyril couldn't believe they were flirting. He leaned over. "Hey, as much as I hate to break this up, I have to get to work. Jamie?"

"Hey, Nick." Jamie ignored Cyril. "I have a question. It's my mother's birthday tomorrow. I wanted to get her a really nice bottle of olive oil for her birthday. Where should I get it?"

Cyril tensed up. Would Nick blow his cover?

"I have absolutely no idea," answered Nick quickly, distracted. "Why would you need olive oil? Isn't it all the same? What's wrong with, like, Wesson oil or something? Mandy!" he yelled for his dog.

Cyril stared, unblinking, desperate to catch Nick's eye.

"I thought you were some kind of gourmet chef or something!" Jamie sounded far less than surprised.

"Uh—uh," Nick stuttered. "Well, I wouldn't say that, no. *Mandy!*" Nick looked over at Cyril, now glaring. Another "Uh," then, "Hey, maybe you should try that place, that, um . . . what's it called? Origami?"

"Origami?" asked Jamie. "Origami?" She turned to Cyril. "Where's that?" Cyril shrugged. Jamie turned to Nick. "Origami?"

"Yeah!" said Nick. "Over at the Hudson Common strip mall. No, wait . . . Oregano. Yeah, that's the place. Try Oregano!"

That was too close.

"Yeah, try Oregano!" yelped Cyril, desperate to go.

"But first, can we mosey already? I need to get to work."

Jamie grabbed the crumpled yellow paper bag off the seat and tossed it out the window at Nick.

"Eat those," said Jamie.

"What are they?" asked Nick, plunging his hand into the bag.

"Pastinos. Or something. Pepitas. Anyway, they're good. But don't drive while you eat them. They're hazardous." She turned on the ignition, revved the engine, and rolled down the window. As she pulled out, she screamed, "Nice pants!" out the window.

Nick's wide grin reminded Cyril of Miss America. Why aren't those two dating? Cyril wondered.

"I suppose you heard about the whole Nick and Rose thing," Jamie said, interrupting Cyril's thoughts.

"The Nick and Rose thing?" Cyril played dumb. Maybe if he played dumb hard enough, it wouldn't be true.

"Yeah. They hooked up after homecoming the other night, you know."

Cyril felt his eyes burn. He'd been struggling to keep his mind off this since last weekend, and the last thing he needed was for Jamie to rub it in. He didn't say anything right away.

"Hello? Cyril? Did you hear me?" Jamie snapped her fingers in front of his face.

"Hooked up?" said Cyril. "What does that even mean? Do you mean they hooked up or *hooked up?*"

"Just hooked up. Nothing major. But still! She was supposed to be my date."

Cyril directed his answer toward Jamie's rearview window, looking straight into the reflection of her eyes. "Yeah, well, I don't care, okay? They can do whatever they want to do." Cyril looked back at his feet.

"Well, I do. This means my chances of ever getting with him are toast," Jamie moaned. "He's off-limits to me now. At least until several days after they break up."

Cyril gave Jamie a sympathy nod. Then quietly, almost to himself, he asked, "Do you think she's happy?"

Jamie inhaled slowly. "Do I think she's happy? Good question." Jamie paused at the stop sign or, more accurately, made a rolling stop. "Hey, I know what's going on."

"What do you mean?" Cyril asked.

"Oh, never mind," Jamie said. "Left here?"

"Left here, yeah," Cyril said. Cyril wasn't sure which "going on" Jamie was referring to. And he was going to keep it that way.

*　　　*　　　*

pepitas (baked pumpkin seeds with cumin)

Cyril was psyched when work was over and he was back at home, in his own kitchen, pacing behind the granite counter, considering what to make his family for dinner, thinking about his audition, and trying not to obsess, when the phone rang.

Oh, please be Rose.

"Have you ever tasted Nick's cheese fondue?" she asked.

Not exactly the conversation starter he was hoping for.

"Um, nope." At least it was an honest answer. He was glad she couldn't see him sweating.

"Hasn't he *ever* cooked for you?"

"No." Cyril flipped on the TV and ripped off his socks.

"It was amazing. It was like liquid and solid at the same time. It was rich, but I didn't get full. I swear there were flavors in there that I've never tasted before. Omigod, and the chocolate fondue. It was unbelievable. And you should have seen the table. Candles everywhere, beautiful silverware. And Mandy was so cute, just lying next to us the whole time. Cyril, he really made the whole night so beautiful. *That's* the way to get a girl, you know? Guys around the world should take a lesson."

"Huh." He hoped his monosyllabic response would kill the conversation. Cyril grabbed a jar of peanut butter out of the fridge and a frozen container filled with some of the chocolate fondue that "Nick" had made the other night. He stuck it in the microwave and set it for one minute. This was painful to listen to, and Cyril needed some serious painkillers.

"Seriously, Cyril," said Rose. "It was magic."

Cyril, red faced now, silently begged the microwave to hurry up.

"Did he say anything about me?" asked Rose.

Bubbling over, Cyril blurted, "No. But who needs boys, anyway, right? At least that's what you were saying last week. And you were making sense then. As opposed to now."

Rose didn't say anything. Cyril dug out a spoonful of peanut butter, dipped it in the warmed-up chocolate, and brought it to his mouth all in one smooth movement. He waited for her response.

"I . . . I guess you're right," said Rose. "Yeah." She was practically whispering now. "You're right."

They were silent for a moment.

"Sorry," said Cyril. "I didn't mean to be harsh. I guess I'm just tired."

"No, I was forgetting all that. I have to be careful," said Rose, still quiet. Then she started crunching.

"What are you eating?" asked Cyril, glad to change the subject.

"Pamplonas. Or pampitos or something. They're seeds with salt and stuff on them."

"Pepitas?"

"Yeah! That's it. Nick gave them to me when I ran into him at the gas station. I guess he made them or something."

Cyril dropped the phone.

"Sorry," he said. "I have a call on the other line."

That was about all Cyril could take. It was time to call the whole charade off. He dialed Nick's number, prepared to tell him off, but it was Nick's mom who answered the phone.

"Hi, Mrs. Garbacchio, is Nick around?"

"No, Cyril," Mrs. Garbacchio said. "I never know where he is."

Cyril waited a second. Mrs. Garbacchio sounded like she was talking through water. It felt like being on the phone was too much responsibility for her. Cyril thanked her and got off the phone. Maybe Cyril was being too harsh. Nick was his best friend, and he had problems of his own.

1 large pumpkin
1 tablespoon butter
2 teaspoons dried cumin powder
coarse salt to taste
2 teaspoons paprika

1. Scoop out all the gunk from the pumpkin into a bowl. (Use a combination of a metal spoon and your hands.) While running cold water over the gunk, separate out the pumpkin seeds. Toss the gunk.
2. Lay the pumpkin seeds in a single layer over paper towels until completely dry. (At least a few hours.)
3. Preheat oven to 300 degrees. Position baking rack in the middle of the oven.
4. Melt the butter in a large Pyrex pitcher in microwave. Stir in 1 teaspoon cumin.
5. Cover a cookie sheet with a single layer of pumpkin seeds. Pour the butter mixture evenly over seeds. Sprinkle with remaining cumin. Swish seeds around to make sure they're evenly coated. Slide the sheet into the oven.
6. Bake for 15–20 minutes, swishing seeds around every 5 minutes to make sure they cook evenly.
7. Remove from oven; sprinkle with salt and paprika while still hot.

8. Let the seeds cool on the sheet. Pour into a bowl or paper bag. Munch away.

Makes about three handfuls

pressed roasted-vegetable sandwiches

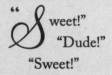"weet!"

"Dude!"

"Sweet!"

"Dude!"

Nick and Cyril never got tired of quoting stupid movie scenes to each other, even first thing in the morning. They didn't miss a beat as Cyril handed Nick a sandwich.

"Sweet!"

"Dude!"

Nick broke the chain when he took a bite.

"Dude, this rules. *Rules!*" Nick said through a mouthful of roasted peppers and garlic. He put his hand up for a high five. "Hey, you got any extra?"

"How come? You anticipating the munchies?"

"Actually, Rose is coming with me today." Nick downed his glass of milk emphatically, like a real milk lover.

"To the city?" Cyril swallowed hard.

"Right you are. The Big Apple. New York, New York. So nice, they named it twice. We're catching the ten fifty-two train . . . a short half hour away!"

"For the whole weekend?" He knew he wouldn't admit it, but he was jealous. *He* wanted to go to New York. Cyril always wanted to go to New York with Nick. Now Rose got to go on Cyril's New York trip and Nick got to assume Cyril's role as a chef. Cyril realized he'd waded deep into the middle of an identity crisis.

Nick waggled his eyebrows. "Can you take care of Mandy for me?"

Cyril took a sip from his cup of coffee. He swallowed, but the coffee found the wrong tube, and Cyril's body began to convulse. He started choking, at first silently, then in a blast of spit.

"Hombre, you okay?" Nick raced to the sink, drew some water, and hopped back to Cyril. "Here! You need the Heimlich?"

Cyril's eyes watered and he grabbed for the counter

to steady himself. He shook his head and held up his hand.

"No," he mouthed, airless. "I'm totally fine." He focused on catching his breath. Cyril caught his breath, took the glass, and had a sip. Then another one. "Seriously, I'm fine." He wrapped another piece of butcher's paper around each already-wrapped-once sandwich. "Well, if you're feeding Rose," he wheezed, "it's a good thing these are vegetarian." Cyril put the sandwiches in a paper bag and handed them to Nick. He then filled another bag with a few fresh kitchen-sink cookies. "Take these, too. I don't need 'em. Have a great time." He ushered his friend through the whiny screen door.

Wiping off the counter, Cyril tried to will the jealousy away. Then again, maybe being in the middle of an identity crisis was better than being the fat guy in the cute-girl/hot-guy/fat-guy love triangle. The more he thought about it, the more pathetic it felt and the more disgusted he was with himself.

The phone rang. "Hello?"

It was Jamie.

"Hey, Cyril. Do you have Nick's phone number? I need to get in touch with Rose, but her phone's shut off."

"Is everything okay?"

"Totally! I just wanna find out what's going on with them!"

"Jamie, they just left like forty-five minutes ago," said Cyril. "Nothing's happened yet! You're a spaz."

"Yeah, right. Gimme a break, Cyril. They've been messing around since they sat down on the train."

It wasn't what Cyril wanted to hear, and it set his mind racing.

Somewhere between Poughkeepsie and Yonkers, with the Hudson speeding past their window, Nick takes his hand from around her shoulder and picks up his well-worn, perfectly rustic leather saddlebag, or is it more of a rucksack? He fishes around inside, never taking his eyes away from Rose's. He pulls out a crumpled paper bag.

"What is it?" she asks, snuggling back into his shoulder.

"It's homemade," he says, pausing to lean down, open his mouth, and nibble on her perfect lower lip. "Mmm," he moans. "Delicious."

Without another word, he takes a butcher's-paper-wrapped bundle out of the paper bag, carefully tears off the end to expose a corner of the pressed sandwich, brings it to his mouth, and takes a hearty bite, closing his eyes and smiling as he chews, slowly, slowly. "Mmm. Almost as good as your lip." He smiles.

Rose, eyes wide, watches him intently, wriggling closer and pressing the entire length of her strong, faded-jeaned thigh along his. She takes off her oval glasses, or maybe the gold wire-rimmed ones, and blinks up at him. She pouts her just bitten and reddening lower lip, moistens it, preparing for a taste of the sandwich as for a kiss. Her lips part as he raises the dense, oily sandwich to it.

She pauses, mouth half open. She looks at him, seeking reassurance. He reads her mind, whispering as he stares into her endless brown eyes, "Don't worry, it's vegetarian."

As she chews, he says, "I love feeding you, Rose. I want to take care of you. I want you to be mine, Rose. You're everything I've ever wanted. Let me take care of you."

Rose listens, trying to think, No, no, that's not what I need. I'm my own woman. I'm independent. I don't want to be taken care of.

But her thoughts never make it out of her mouth because her mouth is overwhelmed with the flavors of the pressed sandwich, stirring surrender in her brain, her throat, her stomach, everywhere. She moves against him, tasting the olive oil and the artichoke. Her face gets flushed. She moans as the cheese runs through her mouth and sighs when the aroma of the roasted-garlic-infused bread coats the back of her tongue.

"Yes," she says. "I'm yours. Take care of me. Take me away and feed me. Feed me your sandwiches. Feed me your kitchen-sink cookies. Feed me you."

This time she raises her lips to his. This time she kisses him, hard. The kiss goes on and on. . . .

"Cyril? The number?" Jamie's voice broke the trance.

"Huh?" asked Cyril, shaking his head back to reality.

"Nick's number!" Jamie sounded insistent. "You need to ease off the pipe, dude."

Cyril forced himself back to wishing he was the one going to New York instead of Rose. It was a far easier kind of angst. And he knew he couldn't put himself through this amount of jealousy for much longer.

2 whole heads garlic

olive oil

2 bell peppers in different colors

3 large portobello mushrooms, sliced into ½-inch strips

coarse salt

1 loaf Italian or French peasant bread

1 bunch spinach, thoroughly washed

fresh mozzarella cheese, sliced

artichoke hearts

marinated sun-dried tomatoes

marinated olives

1 bunch fresh basil

balsamic vinegar

(You can use any combination of veggies you want. You can also add meat to these: smoked turkey, salami, beef, sausages, cured ham, even duck.)

1. Preheat oven to 400 degrees.
2. Slice the garlic heads in half, cutting through the center of the cloves so that all cloves are bisected. Drizzle oil over the garlic, and place the two sides back together. Wrap the garlic in aluminum foil. Place in center of oven, and roast for 40 minutes.
3. Slice the peppers in half; remove the stem and seeds. Drizzle inside and out with olive oil. Put the two halves back together, wrap in alu-

minum foil, and place in oven alongside garlic. Allow to roast for 25 minutes.

4. Remove the garlic and peppers from oven. Do not unwrap. Allow to cool for 10–15 minutes.

5. Over medium-high flame, heat a tablespoon or so of olive oil in a frying pan. Drop in the portobellos and sauté for 8–10 minutes, until they're nice and soft. Remove from heat and let cool.

6. Unwrap the garlic. Squeeze out cloves, mash together with coarse salt, and set aside. Toss foil and garlic paper.

7. Unwrap the peppers. Using a paring knife, scrape off the skin.

8. Slice the bread in half lengthwise. Spread the garlic paste over bottom of bread.

9. Layer all ingredients onto the bread. Start with peppers, then mushrooms, spinach, sun-dried tomatoes, artichoke hearts, mozzarella, olives, basil leaves, etc. Mix and match layers. Drizzle olive oil and balsamic vinegar over veggies. Top with the remaining slice of bread.

10. Wrap sandwich tightly in plastic wrap, and place sandwich in a baking dish. Place a brick or other heavy weight on top of the sandwich so it gets thoroughly pressed down. Stick sandwich in the fridge and press for several hours or preferably overnight. (That baking dish will catch any oil that seeps out.

115

It's a must, or else you'll be scrubbing the refrigerator.)

11. Unwrap the sandwich. Slice into individual pieces and eat.

Makes one large sandwich

(Expect a strong response. People often flip over how good these taste.)

chocolate birthday cake with white frosting

Rose's birthday was tomorrow and Cyril was seated at his computer, racking his brain, trying to compose a birthday message. He wanted to write something personal, something that didn't compromise his dignity, but all he could come up with was, *Please stop making out with Nick.* He was pressing the delete button for the fifteenth time that night when the phone rang. It was a welcome interruption.

"Hello?"

"Hey, dude. I have a question." It was Nick.

"Shoot me," Cyril said, and shook his head. "I mean, shoot."

"What's *baking powder?*" asked Nick.

Cyril was taken aback. "Huh?"

"Is it the same as baking *soda?*" asked Nick, flustered.

"Um, no. Nick, what's going on?" Cyril sensed disaster.

"I'm baking a cake. It's Rose's birthday tomorrow."

"It is?" Cyril feigned ignorance. "What kind of cake?"

"Chocolate," answered Nick proudly.

"And you're not sure what baking powder is?" Cyril prodded. "Don't tell me. You're using Nesquick for cocoa powder. Nick, put down whatever you're doing and turn off the oven before someone gets hurt. You're in way over your head."

"Dude. What am I going to do?"

"Ever heard of a bakery?"

Silence. Cyril knew that this conversation was headed in one direction and one direction only. The only question was how long it would take Nick to get there.

"Cyril?"

"Yes, Nick?"

"How 'bout if I came over and you helped me bake the cake?"

"Wow, Nick. I hadn't thought of that," Cyril said, then paused to milk it a little bit more. He could practically hear Nick whimpering on the other end of the line. Torturing his little Supermodel wasn't as much fun as Cyril thought it would be.

When he could no longer bear the silence, Cyril invited Nick over. Minutes later Nick and Mandy came crashing through the woods and into Cyril's kitchen. Both of them were disheveled and covered with flour. Cyril was waiting in front of the sink, drying his just-washed hands with a dish towel.

"Ten-hut!" Cyril barked. "Now, this is a sorry sight."

This was the signal. Nick picked it up immediately and saluted Cyril, smiling wide. "Sir! Yes, sir!"

"Soldier. Am I to understand that you attempted a chocolate torte with no supervision? Do you realize that you have not been given clearance to attempt to bake on your own?"

"My apologies, sir!"

"Save them. We're going to use this time to clean up the mess you've made. Now, pay close, *close* attention! I'm only going to talk you through this *once*."

"Sir! Yes, sir!"

"I have accessed the main server BRF—Bartholomew Recipe File—for Chocolate Birthday Cake with White Frosting. It indicates that the oven must be preheated to 350 degrees Fahrenheit. Do it now!"

"Sir! Yes, sir!" Nick fumbled with the dials on the oven. "Would you like to check my work, sir?"

Cyril walked over. "You have set it to 380 degrees. Would you like to try again?"

Nick adjusted the dial.

"Now," said Cyril. "Remove two nine-inch circular cake pans from the cabinet to the left of the oven. You'll recognize them as nine inches in diameter because they'll be bigger than anything you've ever seen." He continued, reading from his computer screen, "From the cupboard to my right: cake flour. White granulated sugar. Powdered cocoa. Baking soda. Vanilla. Vegetable oil. White vinegar. Do *not* attempt to retrieve all these items in one trip. Lay them out neatly on the counter." He grabbed the sheet out of the printer and looked over his recipe. "Luckily, I have eggs and butter already at room temperature."

"Sir! Yes, sir!" Nick jumped to his task.

"We'll now assemble all of our ingredients." Cyril liked this teacher–student setup. It made him feel in charge. "Please measure out two tablespoons of vinegar and one half cup of vegetable oil. And one cup of buttermilk."

"Which cup? That coffee cup over by your computer? Or should I use the *Lord of the Rings* cup I got for free when I supersized last night? And tablespoons are the ones you use for cereal, right?"

Cyril shook his head. "Pitiful," he mumbled, chuckling.

By the time the cake was cooled and frosted, Nick might or might not have learned to bake, but they had a picture-perfect two-tiered chocolate cake with white frosting and eighteen white candles (seventeen plus one for good luck, or whatever). There was only one thing missing—a sugar rose for decoration. A rose for Rose. But Nick didn't seem to notice or care. Not that he would.

The next evening Cyril stopped off at Oregano's to pick up Alice's month-old food magazines. Out of curiosity, he stopped by the baking-goods section, where sure enough, there were sugar roses on display. He knew he should let it go, but Rose's cake had been on his mind all day. It would look naked without a rose.

Taking the long way home, Cyril decided to cut through Patriots' Hollow. He knew Nick was planning on presenting the cake to Rose at the picnic area behind the hollow. If Cyril got there in time, he could give Nick the rose. It just didn't feel right to have his cake served unfinished. It wasn't professional.

Cyril crossed into the grove, following the glow of the lighted picnic area. Through the trees, still out of sight of the picnic area, he could see there were people gathered. There was a group of four youngish women, sitting around one picnic table with a bottle of wine, leaning in on one another and chatting the night away. The scene reminded Cyril of *Sex and the City* and made him want to change the channel. But Carrie and company faded quickly when Cyril caught sight of a figure coming down the path to the picnic area and lost his breath.

Rose.

She was in a pale pink cable-knit sweater and a flowered gauze skirt, and she looked more beautiful than ever. She was also much earlier than Cyril had expected. Which meant it was too late for Cyril to give the rose to Nick. Without looking like a complete dork in front of Rose, that is.

Cyril turned around to leave but once again was unable to pull himself away from the sight of Nick and Rose. He'd never thought of himself as a voyeur before, but these last few weeks had been full of surprises. Why not watch? He'd already withstood more pain than he'd ever imagined, and he didn't see it all ending anytime soon. The scene was both perfect and awful.

There was Nick, seated at the farthest table, directly behind a snow-white two-tiered cake, ablaze with white candles, and there was Rose, her diaphanous skirt flowing behind her as she walked toward him. Even the *Sex and the City* girls went silent. As she approached, Nick began to sing. Not in an annoying, embarrassing way, but in a quiet, intimate way, with lots of breath and pauses.

"Happy birthday to you, happy birthday to you . . ." Cyril thought Nick's gift for singing almost made up for his complete lack of ability in the kitchen.

Rose folded into his arms as Nick finished. He planted a quick kiss on her lips, then cupped her face for a deeper one. But Rose smiled and quickly turned toward the cake. "Wow! Is this for me?" Then she sat down across from Nick. Not next to him. Cyril took a step back. He had to get out of there. This wasn't right.

Across from, not next to . . .

Cyril took one more look behind him before

walking back home through the woods. He could see the disappointment in his buddy's face. He felt bad for Nick. But not that bad. He hoped the two of them enjoyed the cake. He hoped they'd eat the whole thing and be way, way too tired to do anything else. The rose was still in the bag, and he ate it while he walked. He told himself the sugar would keep him strong.

Cake:

2 cups sifted cake flour

1 cup sugar

1 cup unsweetened cocoa

2 teaspoons baking soda

1 teaspoon salt

2 large eggs, at room temperature

2 teaspoons vanilla extract

½ cup vegetable oil

1 cup buttermilk

2 tablespoons white vinegar

1 cup boiling water

1. Preheat oven to 350 degrees. Grease and lightly flour two 9-inch cake pans.
2. Sift together all the dry ingredients (flour, sugar, cocoa, baking soda, salt) into a large mixing bowl.
3. Whisk together the eggs, vanilla, oil, and buttermilk in a small bowl.
4. Make a small well in the dry ingredients. Fill the well with the egg mixture. Using a plastic spatula or wooden spoon, slowly incorporate egg mixture into dry ingredients. Add vinegar; mix well.
5. When the batter is almost smooth, pour hot water into batter, stirring as you pour.
6. Carefully pour the batter into cake pans. Bake on the center rack of the oven for 20–25 minutes. After 12 minutes, rotate the pans for even

baking. The cake layers are done when a tooth-pick inserted into the exact middle of one of the cake pans comes out almost clean.

7. Leave cake in pans and cool on rack for 15 minutes. Then turn cake out of pans and continue cooling on rack until completely cooled. Meantime, make the frosting.

Frosting:

2 cups powdered sugar, plus extra as needed

½ stick unsalted butter, softened

3–4 tablespoons whole milk, plus extra if needed

2 teaspoons vanilla extract

1 pinch salt

1. Sift the powdered sugar into a medium mixing bowl.
2. Using an electric beater on medium speed, beat butter into the powdered sugar until just combined.
3. Increase beater speed to medium high, then add milk, vanilla, and salt. Beat until smooth. If needed, add more sugar or milk.
4. Frost the cake liberally.

Serves twelve

(No comment.)

m & m brownies with caramel drizzle

"*I* don't get it. I mean, that cake was *awesome!*"
Nick tripped alongside Cyril as they fought the
tide of students sweeping down the main second-floor
hallway of NHPR. "But it didn't work."

"What do you mean, didn't work?" asked Cyril
impatiently. He was trying to shake the rain off his
slicker, but so was every other kid in the overcrowded
hallway, and it was just making everyone wetter.

"I mean," Nick said. "Oh, you know what I mean."

"You mean you didn't score last night? You mean
the cake didn't seal the deal for you?"

Just then Christina Cartagena passed by and scowled
at Cyril. Clearly she didn't approve of his word choice.

"Not even a little. Not that I was looking for all

that. I'm just saying she barely even kissed me. And it was her birthday!" Nick spoke as if he'd suffered a grave injustice.

Cyril picked up the pace. "That's nice. See you later."

Cyril stopped in front of the biology lab. Two steps later he was face-to-face with Rose. She looked unrested and sleepy. There was a half-eaten cinnamon bun in her hand.

"Hi, Rosie," said Nick. "How's my girl? Whatcha got there? A sticky bun?" Cyril turned around to see Nick bend his knees, wrap his lean runner's arms around her, and lift her off the ground. "My favorite sticky buns are right here." Cyril turned back around and moved off, but not before he saw Nick grab both of Rose's cheeks and heard him repeat, "Mmm. Sticky buns. Thanks for making me the happiest man at NHPR."

Rose squawked, "Ew! Go away!" She squirmed away with a laugh, but Cyril could tell she wasn't amused. Offended was more like it.

"See ya later, Sticky, see ya, Cyril." Nick was grinning more stupidly than ever. "I'll let you two Einsteins get to class. I've got to get to remedial science."

Cyril stepped into the lab and took his seat. Rose

stumbled behind him, slamming her books onto the counter. She pulled back a sloppy ponytail and secured it with a rubber band from her wrist. "I have a zit," she said. "I need a nap. I don't know what I'm doing. I hate boys." She struggled through a smile. "And I'm wearing my ugly glasses today." She sighed and looked over at Cyril. "How are you?"

Cyril didn't know how to feel because he didn't know what was going on. He was glad that Rose wasn't all glowing and dreamy after her date with Nick. The fact that she was in a horrible mood was comforting. Cyril wasn't sure what to do. Should he probe? Should he dig?

He played it safe. "I'm fine. I'm happy to see you."

Rose sighed and dropped her head on the countertop, banging it slowly and dramatically against the surface.

"Are you okay?" asked Cyril.

"I don't know." Rose rested her cheek on the counter. "I don't know what's wrong."

Just then reliable, annoying Brandon Keifler, baseball cap on backward, passed their desk. "Long night, Rose?" He snickered and kept walking, not even waiting for a rebuttal.

"Shut up, Brandon," she hissed back. Then to Cyril, "Correction. I do know what's wrong. Boys."

"Rose," said Cyril. "Forget Brandon. He's a dick."

"Not just Brandon. All boys suck," said Rose. "All of them."

Cyril cleared his throat.

"Present company excluded, of course," said Rose. She reached over and rubbed Cyril's back. "I mean boy-boys. Not you."

For better or for worse, Cyril was used to this kind of comment. "Did something happen with Nick?"

"No. Yes. Maybe. I don't know. He's a nice guy, but I just don't know what I want. I'm in over my head. I mean, of course I want to be in love. Everyone does. But I just don't know about having another *boyfriend*. The last one sucked. And boys, they're like aspirin or something. They make you feel better for a while, but then they cause all kinds of side effects, you know? Like, Nick never would admit this, but I got the feeling that he expected something from me last night. He made me a cake, and that was nice. But then he was acting like that made him entitled to . . . well . . . you know what I mean. I didn't even want to kiss him or sit near him."

Cyril kept quiet as Rose continued. "Or maybe he didn't expect anything. Maybe I just thought he did. I don't know. Ugh, this is too much. I'm just getting over Brandon. I'm not ready for all this."

Cyril was riveted, unblinking.

"Maybe it's all the food," she said. "His food is just so incredible. I mean, those kitchen-sink cookies. How many boys do you know that can make cookies that taste so good? I think about those cookies every night. I feel like that *says* something about a person, you know. Like that they're really passionate."

"But then he goes and calls my butt 'sticky buns' and ruins everything. He doesn't know me well enough to be talking about my butt." She stopped. "What am I talking about? Butts and sticky buns? Ugh. I just . . . I don't know what's wrong with me, Cyril."

He didn't say anything, waiting for more. Rose quickly sputtered, "I don't know what else to say." Rose closed her eyes. "Cyril, I need you."

Cyril never thought of Rose needing him. But he liked the way it sounded. *I need you*—he savored those words, willing time into slow motion.

But she was still talking. "I need a pep talk. I need you to tell me I'm not a freak, and I'm going to be all right, and I'm not out of control or anything and all that stuff. And—"

"And?" She *needed* him.

"And that I'm strong and, I don't know. Just tell me I'm not out of my mind." But just then the bell rang and the room quieted down.

Cyril leaned in to Rose's ear. He spoke softly. "Rose, you just said it for yourself. You don't need a pep talk from me. But I'll say it, anyway: I am reasonably, no, totally certain that you are *not* out of your mind. You're one of the good ones, Rose. I'm sure of it." He smiled at her. "I promise."

Rose opened her eyes and smiled up at Cyril sideways. "You're the only one who sees me, Cyril." She grabbed his wrist. "I love you."

Cyril was transported. Spellbound. Did she really just say that? This was a dream. He reached into his bag because he'd made some brownies and he wanted to give Rose one, but then he thought better of it. This wasn't a food moment.

She patted his hand. "Oh my God. Do you know that you're only the second guy in my life that I've ever said that to? How funny is that!"

Cyril's face flushed. "Funny," he said with a chuckle, hoping to appear nonchalant. He swallowed, but he didn't like the taste.

1 14-ounce can sweetened condensed milk

1 stick butter

1 12-ounce bag unsweetened or semisweet chocolate bits, frozen

2 cups sugar

2 teaspoons real vanilla extract

4 large eggs

1 cup all-purpose flour

1 cup M&M's, plain or peanut, depending on your preference, frozen

1. Preheat oven to 400 degrees. Pour the sweetened condensed milk into a glass pie plate and cover with aluminum foil. Place the pie plate into a large roasting pan, then pour hot tap water into the roasting pan, deep enough to come halfway up the side of the pie plate. (This is called a *bain-marie*; it helps keep the caramel from burning.) Bake for 1 hour. Check frequently and add water to the *bain-marie* if the level drops below halfway up the pan.

2. While the caramel sauce is baking, line a 9-by-13–by-2-inch baking pan with aluminum foil. Let a little hang over the ends.

3. Put the butter and half of the frozen chocolate bits into a microwave-safe glass pitcher and microwave on medium until melted, about 2½ minutes total. Don't let it bubble. Whisk gently

to remove any lumps, then pour chocolate mixture into a large bowl. Let stand for 5 minutes to cool. Add sugar and vanilla. Stir well.

4. In a small bowl lightly break up the eggs with a fork. Add to the chocolate mixture and blend thoroughly.

5. Stir in the flour. Mix just until blended; don't overwork it.

6. Fold in the remaining chocolate bits and frozen M&M's.

7. Using a plastic spatula, scrape the batter into the pan and spread evenly. Turn oven down to 350 degrees and bake alongside caramel for about 25 minutes, until a toothpick inserted into the middle comes out almost clean, but not quite. Remove from oven and place pan on a cooling rack.

8. Remove the sweetened condensed milk from the oven, uncover, and stir. It may need 5 more minutes.

9. While the caramel sauce is cooking, carefully lift brownies out of their pan by the aluminum foil handles. Cut into generous-sized bars and drizzle with caramel sauce.

Makes about 12 brownies

(Awesome on good days. Even better on bad days.)

spicy tomato soup

"Where've you been?" Rose asked Jamie. They were coming out of school at the end of what had been far too long a day. Rose had been listening to a Grateful Dead CD she'd borrowed from her mom, and she'd been deep into an old fantasy of hers, about what it might've been like to be her age back in the sixties, when people were so much nicer to one another and the music was so much better. But then she'd seen Jamie, who had come slamming out of school in some kind of rush. Rose thought that Jamie, who was dressed in head-to-toe Lycra, would not have fit into the sixties at all.

"Rose—I'm so glad I ran into you," Jamie said. Rose smiled. They'd seen each other so little lately, and Rose was suddenly kind of hopeful that they could hang out now. She should be spending way more time with girls.

"Me, too," Rose said. "We should do something together, tonight, maybe? I hope you're not mad at me about the dance."

"You mean for leaving me and running off with my one true love?" Jamie asked. "I am. But I'll get over it. Besides, I'm not so sure he's all that worth it. There's something I have to tell you, but I don't want you to get all, like, sensitive about it."

Jamie sat down next to one of the concrete lions on either side of the school steps. Rose stood in front of her. Suddenly Rose felt kind of nervous.

"What?" Rose asked. She heard strains of "Sugar Magnolia" leaking out of her earphones, and she reached down and flipped off the music.

"It's just—you know how Nick cooks for you? How it's so amazing when he does that?"

"Yeah," Rose said. She was getting a very creepy feeling. As if Jamie were going to tell her something that she should have known all along.

"Well, there's no way Nick cooks like that. He knows as much about how to cook as I do about long-term relationships. He may serve the food. But somebody else cooks it."

"Who?" Rose asked. She thought her voice sounded far away, but then she realized she was only whispering.

"Cyril," Jamie said. "I'm sorry."

"That's impossible. Look, I'm not mad at you or anything. But if I didn't know better, I might think you were jealous of me and Nick," Rose said, tugging at the tiny silver bells that hung from the drawstring of her gauze skirt.

"Well, I am jealous of you and Nick, but that has nothing to do with what I'm telling you. It's not like I'm going to go all *Swim Fan* on you guys," said Jamie.

Rose felt terrible. She'd never thought of Jamie as someone who could feel jealous over a guy. What was *one* guy to the J. Lo of New Hyde Park Regional?

"James, I'm sorry. Do you want to talk about it?"

Jamie slapped the concrete lion's back and laughed as hard as she had laughed the time Rose left the house wearing panty hose with her Birkenstocks. "Rosie, get over yourself. I don't need to *talk*. You're dating Nick, and I'm hanging out at Vassar and getting juniors to buy me beers at Mugs. Life's like that sometimes. But you need to listen to me about the cooking thing."

Rose was petting the lion's mane. "I know that's not true. 'Cause if it was . . ."

"What?" Jamie said. She'd gotten up slowly, and now she was leaning against the lion on his other side.

"If it was . . . I couldn't talk to either of those guys ever again. I'd be so angry, I don't know what I'd do. Doesn't matter, though, 'cause there's no way Cyril would do that to me. I trust him way too much, and I can't imagine he'd ever lie to me like that."

"Even if it's what he thought you wanted?" Jamie asked.

"But I wouldn't want that," Rose said. "Nobody likes being made a fool of."

"I shouldn't have told you," Jamie said. "Forget it. I don't know it for sure. Do you want a ride?"

"No, I think I'm going to walk," Rose said. "Anyway, I hear that lately you're not so hot behind the wheel." Rose put her headphones back on and walked away. She thought, *There's no way Jamie could be right.*

No way.

"What?"

"This soup," Nick said as he took another slurp.

"What?" Cyril was just fishing. He knew how good his spicy tomato soup was. How it filled the kitchen with a rich, sweet, deep, tongue-coating tomato aroma. And how the rest of his family loved it, too. Cyril was hoping to find a variation on it that would work for his AICA audition.

"It's good."

"Thanks."

Cyril thought it was another one of their perfect nonconversations, but apparently Nick was just getting started. "I can't figure out what's up with Rose. I'm not sure if she's pissed at me or what."

"Really?" was about the best Cyril could do. Inside, part of him jumped for joy, while the other part prepared to play the concerned best friend.

"Mmm," Cyril's mother said, still in her nursing whites and squishy shoes. She wore a name tag that read LAURIE, and her bright red curls made the circles under her eyes appear darker. "Smells good, honey. Can I take some up to your father?"

"Hi, Mrs. Bartholomew," said Nick.

"Hi, Nick. I didn't see you there. You getting something to eat?"

"Sure am. Thanks."

"Cyril, send some soup home with Nick. I'm gonna go lie down." She turned back to the hallway.

"Wait, Mom. Here." Cyril held up a tray with two bowls. "For you and Dad."

Mrs. Bartholomew stopped, looked at Cyril, and smiled gently. "We'd starve without you, you know." She reached out and mussed his hair.

"Who's Laurie?" asked Cyril.

"Who?"

"Your name tag."

"Oh my God. I'm wearing Laurie MacPheirson's name tag. I must have switched mine with hers in the locker room. Someone get me to bed."

Cyril squirmed away. "Have a good sleep." Mrs. Bartholomew nodded and backed into the hall. Cyril grabbed the remote and flipped on the TV. Emeril was making a glazed ham.

"So wait," said Nick. "Has Rose said anything to you about being pissed at me?" He grabbed the remote and pressed mute.

"Not really."

"C'mon. Is she mad at me?"

Cyril stared down his friend for a silent moment. "Seriously, dude, I don't know." Pause. "I don't think so."

"I just feel like she's not into it anymore. Like, up until the birthday cake, I could tell she liked me back.

140

But now she's just like, 'Whatever.' She hardly even kissed me on her birthday."

Cyril didn't know what to say. He looked at his hands and wished he was kneading something.

"Sounds like you two need to get a little sumpin' sumpin' going," Mrs. Bartholomew chirped from the hallway.

"What did you say?" Cyril's face turned ghost white.

Mrs. Bartholomew poked her head in. "Oh, I really don't have a clue. Something I heard on TV. Just liked the sound of it." She turned around and headed up the stairs. "Sorry, guys, I'll take my eavesdropping old self up the stairs."

Cyril raised his finger to his temple and rotated it in a circle as he mouthed the word *cuckoo* to Nick. But still, he was unable to erase his mortification. Not only was his mother trying to sabotage any hope he had for a love life, she was also talking dirty talk to his friends. He listened with relief as she padded up the stairs.

And then with fear as she padded back down.

"But Nick, sweetheart, don't be afraid to dazzle her."

Is she kidding?

"Um, thanks," Nick said.

"Good night, Mom."

Mrs. Bartholomew was in desperate need of a vacation. And as far as Cyril was concerned, she could leave right now.

Cyril and Nick waited in silence until they heard the door to Mrs. Bartholomew's bedroom close.

"Cyril? Do you think your mom's on the right track? Nothing I've done so far has been *dazzling*. I've done fun, and adventurous, and romantic, but not dazzling. I'm not even sure I know what *dazzling* is."

Cyril, hoping for distraction, flipped to the Discovery Channel.

"Awesome. *Aliens*. Dude, I saw this last night. You have to see the way these lights hung in the sky over Tucson for, like, a week."

"I'm asking because you seem to really *get* Rose. She has a lot of respect for you, Cyril. She talks about you all the time. She really trusts you."

"Well, we're friends. Lab partners."

"Yeah, but it's more than that. I don't think I'll ever have what you have with her." Nick took another slurp of soup. "I'm not sure what I did, but whatever it was, you would never do it. You'd know better." Nick looked at his feet. "I think she'd like me more if I were more like you."

"Yeah, right." Cyril stood up and walked back to his stove. *That* was a laugh. The last person Rose would want to date would be Cyril.

"Especially if I could cook," said Nick. "I mean, she still won't shut up about those kitchen-sink cookies. What do you think I should do?"

Cyril didn't say a word. Nick stood up and joined Cyril behind the stove. "So, come on, man. Everything was so perfect at that fondue dinner. And she loved those pressed sandwiches. And the cake."

"But you said things didn't go well with the cake," Cyril spat back.

"Naw, the cake wasn't the problem. It was me that was the problem. So, my man, now what?" Nick did that eyebrow-wiggle thing. It was his way of saying, "Please do the thing I want you to do, even though you don't want to."

And it wasn't just that Cyril didn't *want* to. He was also afraid of getting caught. The birthday cake was one thing, but those three-course meals were pretty risky. Especially now that Jamie was quite possibly catching on.

"No way. I'm done cooking for you. It's getting dangerous, man. Aren't you afraid of getting caught?"

"Not if we're careful."

Cyril debated telling Nick about his conversation with Jamie and that he was afraid she knew what was going on. Instead, he opted to keep things simple. "Can't you do something romantic that doesn't involve food?"

"No. I think the food is what romances her. If that makes any sense. Food can have that effect on people. Have you ever heard of aphrodisiacs?"

Once again Cyril couldn't believe his ears. Did Nick actually think there was *anything* about food he'd heard of before Cyril had heard of it? Or maybe Nick categorized aphrodisiacs under the heading of "love," not "food," and that's why he felt he had to ask. Because Cyril was ignorant in matters of love. This night was getting more insulting by the minute.

"Dude, aphrodisiacs don't really work. That's a myth," said Cyril.

"Well, maybe they only work if you want them to work. Anyway, you know what I mean." Nick grabbed Cyril's shoulder and looked him in the eye. "Please. I think it's my last chance. This is make-it-or-break-it time. Please?"

He got my girl, now he's after Aphrodisia?
"But . . ."

144

"Please? I need you."

Cyril wanted to protest, *Now you need me? You need me, Rose needs me, everyone seems to need me. What about what I need?* But part of Cyril was touched. Nick had probably never uttered the words *I need you* before to anyone and meant it. Besides, for all the pity parties Cyril had thrown himself over the last few weeks, he had a lot to be thankful for. He knew where he was headed in life, and he had his family's full support. But what did Nick have? Maybe Nick got to have Rose because Cyril got to have cooking. And maybe it wasn't up to Cyril to decide who got what.

"Invite her over for dinner. Tomorrow night." Cyril spoke quickly, before he had time to change his mind.

Nick grabbed Cyril's shoulders and shook him, hard. "I love this man!" he yelled. "You're the greatest friend a guy could have."

But Cyril didn't feel like he was the greatest friend. The greatest friend would be enthusiastic about helping his friend. The greatest friend would jump at the chance. Cyril had to be begged.

"So what's for dinner?" Nick asked as he washed out his soup bowl.

Now was Cyril's chance to be a *great* friend. "Nothing too fancy. Just a little meal I like to refer to as Aphrodisia."

It wasn't exactly how he'd pictured finally making the aphrodisiac dinner, but somehow it made sense. Besides, Cyril had no reason to save it anymore. It was pretty clear that he'd never have the opportunity to use it on Rose himself.

8 plum tomatoes
olive oil
1 medium onion, chopped
salt and pepper
1 jalapeño pepper, chopped
3 cloves garlic, chopped
hot red pepper flakes
1 cup good-quality chicken stock
1 bay leaf
1 lemon
balsamic vinegar
½ bunch fresh basil

1. Preheat the broiler.
2. Cut all the tomatoes in half and place skin side up in a roasting pan. Brush with olive oil. Slide the roasting pan under the broiler and broil until skins are charred. Flip tomatoes with tongs and continue to broil until the other sides are charred as well. Turn off the broiler, then set tomatoes aside to cool.
3. In a nice big soup pot, over medium heat, warm up 3 tablespoons olive oil. Toss in the onion, salt, and pepper and stir until onions are nice and soft and just barely turning brown, about 8 minutes. Toss in the jalapeño and continue to cook, about 4 minutes. Next throw in the garlic and red pepper flakes and cook 2 minutes more.

4. Dump the tomatoes into the pot and break them up with a wooden spoon. Pour in the chicken stock. Add a bay leaf. Simmer everything at a very low boil for about a half hour.
5. Turn off the heat and let the soup cool down, covered, for about 15 minutes. Dig through and find the bay leaf; discard it. Pour soup into a blender or food processor with steam-release opening opened and puree for 2 minutes.
6. Strain the soup through a sieve to remove bits of skin.
7. Warm the soup up before serving. Serve with a squeeze of lemon juice or a drizzle of balsamic vinegar and two or three basil leaves torn up over the top.

Dinner serves two

(Watch out! It's so good, you'll give out your secrets.)

aphrodisia

Rose pulled her mother's Saab into Nick's driveway, flicked off the headlights, and stepped out. Nick was waiting for her.

"Hi, beautiful," said Nick. "Fig?" He held out a big red glass tumbler full of figs. "You'll like these." Rose cocked her head and looked at him sideways. She wasn't wearing glasses. Her ponytail, extra high and extra tight tonight, danced behind her. Cyril, hidden from view as he watched them from Nick's kitchen window, softened at the knees.

"You look dangerous," said Nick.

Rose smiled, then took a fig and a bite. "Mmm. What's on this? There's like a powder coating it." Rose tasted again. "Is it some kind of spice?"

Cyril held his breath.

Nick stumbled. "Uh . . . you tell me." Flirting now, he put his arm around her waist. "What does it taste like?"

"Tastes like . . . tastes good." Rose smiled, flirting back. They rounded the corner of the house, and Cyril changed windows. He gasped at his first full sight of Rose. He'd never seen a skirt that short on her before, or a sweater that tight. Not to mention boots that high. This was the first time Cyril had ever seen her out of her hippie-chick threads. Tonight she was going for full-on mod. Her beauty nearly knocked Cyril off balance.

Nick walked behind her, obviously agog. Mandy bounced around them, yapping gently.

"Careful," said Nick. "Those are aphrodisiacs." Cyril imagined Nick wiggling his eyebrows as he said it and cringed.

"Ha. Yeah, right," said Rose. "Aphrodisiacs. Gimme a break." She popped another fig in her mouth.

Cyril remembered what Nick said about aphrodisiacs working if you wanted them to and wondered if it was true.

Just as they stepped out of view, Cyril heard Rose

gasp, "Wow." Cyril knew she was reacting to the patio, which was awash in Moroccan red and gold and utterly spectacular. The table was crowded with platters and bowls and richly draped with layers of exotic fabric. There were eight black candles in mismatched brass candlesticks, burning gently. Overstuffed cushions were scattered on the floor, with woven covers like Persian carpets, and there was an ornate brass-and-turquoise tea tray with cut-glass teacups set in tiny brass bases with curlicue handles.

There was food everywhere. A red lacquer bowl was half filled with what looked like a bright orange dip. Another held a mound of artichoke hearts. A small brass plate framed a scoop of a caramel-brown paste with white flakes over the top. There was a mahogany salad bowl filled with shiny leaves of arugula. A marble slab was covered with eight perfect chocolates. A stack of torn flat bread. An aqua-blue mosaic lazy Susan piled high with what looked like violet and yellow flower petals, only sparkly.

"Wow," she said again. By now Cyril was watching from the sliding doors, melting.

Nick set down the red glass tumbler of figs on the only spare spot on the table.

Cyril noticed the music floating over the scene. Exotic, rhythmic, but soothing. Just then, as if her brain were totally in sync with Cyril's, Rose asked, "What's that music? Arabic?"

"Yeah," said Nick. "It's the new Cheb Mami CD. Isn't it awesome?"

"Can you eat those?" Rose pointed at the flower petals.

"Well, um." Nick stumbled again. "Well, that just depends on how adventurous you are." Nick grinned and tweaked Rose's nose.

"I'm adventurous," Rose said. "I just want to believe that people are who they say they are. But if I can trust them, that's all that matters."

That kinda came out of nowhere. Cyril wondered what Rose was getting at. And whether Nick had even caught her comment.

"Sure," Nick said. "Sit! I'll be right back." He kissed her hand, then backed toward the door, slid it open, and collapsed inside. His eyes widened when he saw Cyril, and he inhaled to speak.

Cyril put his finger to his mouth. *Don't speak!* They walked silently to the kitchen.

"Good that you're still here," whispered Nick. "I thought you were gone! Can you eat the flowers?"

"Yes, you can eat the flowers," said Cyril, pouring out two tall glasses of hibiscus tea and handing them to Nick. "I'm just about out of here."

Just then they heard Rose scream. Not a scared scream, more of a laugh-scream. "Mandy! Omigod! Nick! Come here, hurry! Mandy!"

Balancing the tea, Nick raced to the patio. "What's wrong?" he yelled back. "Are you okay?"

Cyril followed slowly, in the shadows. Rose was standing up, holding an empty brass plate.

"She—I—she—omigod—" Rose started laughing. "I'm sorry. I'm sorry. I'm not laughing."

"Rose! What happened? Mandy, what's wrong?" Nick handed Rose a glass. "Tea."

"She ate a whole plate of food! Nick, she cleaned it in one bite!" Rose's laugh went from a giggle to a belly laugh. "You should have seen it! She came out of nowhere and jumped up on the table and like . . ." Rose's voice evaporated. She was breathless but laughing with gusto. "She—she—aha-ha-ha-ha! What did she eat, anyway?"

"Where is she?" asked Nick, sounding slightly panicked.

"I think she just walked out onto the grass,

probably to puke. Aw, poor thing. She'll be okay, right?"

"Of course." Nick turned to the yard, distracted. "Mandy! Come here, girl!" he yelled out into the darkness, but he couldn't see her anywhere. He stepped out onto the grass. "Mandy! Come here, baby girl!"

"What do you think she ate?" asked Rose. "What was on that plate?"

"There's no telling," said Nick. "Could have been anything." Luckily he just sounded confused rather than clueless. "I'm gonna go find her. Rose, can you hold down the fort? Promise me you won't move. I'll be back in a flash." He grinned at her. "Drink your tea and enjoy Cheb Mami."

And he was gone.

There stood Cyril, just inside the still unclosed sliding door, out of view, silent, alone. And there, just outside the still unclosed door, sat Rose, well lit, beautiful, alone. Cyril had a perfect view of her perfect profile. He stayed still for a few minutes, watching.

He watched Rose begin to eat. First she slathered a piece of dessert bread with the chickpea dip Cyril had prepared earlier. He imagined the smooth, sweet, garlicky paste coating the back of her throat.

Next he saw her reach for an artichoke heart, which

she carefully pressed between her tongue and the roof of her mouth. Cyril imagined the earthy, rich flavor. "Mmm . . ." she purred as she kicked off her boots and had a sip of hibiscus tea. Then she reached into the salad bowl and wrapped a piece of blood orange in a leaf of arugula. Cyril held his breath as she got up and walked to the edge of the deck.

"Nick?" she half yelled. "You there?"

There was no answer. Rose went back for another bite of the chickpeas. She picked at her teeth with her fingernail. "Where is he?" she muttered to herself.

Just as Cyril thought she was about to sit back down, Rose turned suddenly toward the sliding doors.

Cyril took in his breath and held it. It was too late for him to make a move. How could he have let this happen? He had completely lost sight of his purpose. He was supposed to be cooking, not spying. Rose stepped inside and felt along the wall for a light switch. She found it quickly and flicked it, drenching Cyril in light. He was busted.

"Cyril!" She looked both upset and suspicious. "What are you doing here?"

"Rose! Hi! I, uh . . . I didn't know you were here! I needed the cheat book for Final Fantasy X, so I just came in. I thought you guys were going out tonight!" Cyril was thinking fast and lying faster, but it seemed to be working.

"Oh, that's funny, I didn't know you were into Final Fantasy," said Rose.

He wasn't. It was just the first excuse that came to mind. Cyril went for his jacket. "Oh. Well, I gotta go."

Rose reached for Cyril's hand. "Wait. You should see this. It's beautiful."

Cyril let Rose lead him outside. "Wow," he said. "It's amazing."

"Isn't it incredible? Look at all this food. Look at the candles!" She pointed around the patio. "It's all so beautiful."

"Yeah," said Cyril, although all he was looking at was Rose. The low, flickering candlelight bathed her in a sexy, golden red glow. She was breathtaking. All of Cyril's worries over getting busted fell to the wayside as he took Rose in.

"Yeah," said Rose, turning toward Cyril. She looked at him and gasped. "Cyril! I, uh . . . wow, you look *great!*"

"What?" Cyril hadn't heard those words lately. Or maybe ever. He looked down to see what she was looking at. He was wearing a sweatshirt and jeans. Not exactly dressed up or anything. "Uh, thanks." He kept his eyes on his shoes.

"No, seriously. I never realized how handsome you are," said Rose. Cyril was tempted to believe her, but he couldn't. Maybe it was the aphrodisiacs talking.

But I don't believe in aphrodisiacs.

"Where's Nick?" he asked.

"Mandy ate something and got sick and ran off. He's out there somewhere, looking for her." Rose swept her hand across the lawn. "It's this whole big *thing*. Anyway, you have to try this stuff. I don't know what it is, but you slather it all over bread and, man, it's so good."

"No, I don't want to crash your date," said Cyril.

"Please stay. It's all right," said Rose. "I mean, who knows when Nick'll be back—Mandy was really sick. And I could use the company. Besides, he trusts you, right?" she said with a wink.

Cyril had never seen Rose wink before. What had gotten into her?

"Wow, this is great out here."

"Yeah, quite a spread, isn't it? Pretty amazing. Too bad Nick's not here," she said with the kind of upward lilt that would, under any other circumstance, suggest flirtation. She handed Cyril a bit of dessert bread. "Here. Sit down. Slather this with that."

Cyril, undeserving, sat down and slathered. Rose sat next to him. Almost on top of him, in fact.

"Rose," he said. "If you want to go home, I can hang out here and wait for Nick. I mean, I can't imagine this is what you had in mind for your date." He bit into the chickpea slather. Perfect, as expected.

"And let you eat all this food alone? Are you crazy?" Rose laughed. "Here, you have to try these artichoke hearts. Omigod. They taste like, I don't even know. Like heaven. I can't explain, you have to try it. And the salad. Cyril, try this." Rose was moving slowly, savoring every morsel, not speeding from dish to dish. "Hey, you want to hear something funny?"

"Okay," said Cyril, bracing.

"These are all aphrodisiacs," said Rose, sparkling.

"What?" Cyril wished he knew how to sparkle back.

"Yeah, I never believed in them, but now I'm starting to wonder." She had another sip of tea. "You'd better watch out!" She poked his leg with her bootless toe.

Were they working? This was too incredible.

"Maybe we should save some food for Nick," said Cyril.

"Nah. He's probably at Burger King right now," said Rose, laughing, rather heartily, at her own joke. "I mean, come on, he didn't even know whether the flowers were edible."

What happened to "His food is so incredible"? She must be on to us. Thanks, Jamie. Cyril speared another blood orange and watched closely as Rose practically made out with a fig, then reached for another artichoke heart.

Midmouthful, Rose grabbed Cyril's wrist and asked, brown eyes intense, "Why don't you have a girlfriend, Cyril?"

Cyril wasn't sure how to answer, so he settled on, "I don't know." It seemed the easiest way to get out of it. He grabbed a fig.

"Seriously, Cyril. I mean, you're the kind of guy a girl can really *talk* to. You *listen.* You *understand.*" Rose picked up a chocolate bonbon, raised it to her lips, closed her eyes, and popped it in her mouth. "Mmm." She licked the chocolate off her fingers. "Cyril. Oh my God. This is *so* amazing."

When she opened her eyes, she aimed them directly

at Cyril's. Rose reached back and took out her ponytail. Cyril was amazed. He thought he already knew how beautiful her hair was, but when she ran her fingers through it and shook it free, it caught the candlelight, and it was as if Cyril were seeing it for the first time. He wanted to feel it on his face.

Rose held his eyes as she reached over and took up a flower petal from the pile. "If you're feeling adventurous, you should eat one of these. You knew you could eat them, didn't you, Cyril?" She slipped it into her mouth, closing her eyes. "Mmm." She threw her leg into his lap, stopping his heart. Cyril felt his eyes flicker when he saw her licking her lips. He was still staring at her mouth when she opened her eyes, lashes moving slowly. He couldn't believe this was happening. Either Nick *was* right about aphrodisiacs working if you wanted them to or Cyril was the object of an elaborate sting operation. "Cyril, here." She held one up to his mouth to feed it to him. "Open your mouth and close your eyes, and you will get a big surprise," mouthed her lips as she moved toward him.

He closed his eyes and tasted the flower. "Yum," he moaned.

When he opened his eyes, Rose was staring at him.

"You know, Rose," he said, "I should get out of here. I'm getting in the way of your date."

"Cyril," said Rose. "Look around. You're my date now." She pulled in close and held his gaze intently. "And these aphrodisiacs are definitely working for me. Are they working for you, Cyril?" she asked, cupping his chin in her hand.

Cyril didn't know what to say or do. He was as close to Rose as he'd ever been, and there was nothing pleasant about it. Before he could make a move in either direction, the sliding door burst open.

"Nick!" yelled Cyril and Rose in tandem.

"Hi, Cyril. What are you doing here?" Nick looked nervous. "You moving in on my date, man?" Nick laughed, but Cyril could tell it was forced.

"I, uh . . ." Cyril caught his breath. He looked around and realized Rose's leg was thrown up over his own. He wriggled free and stood up. "I was just looking for a cheat sheet, and I bumped into Rose."

"Sorry, we ate everything," said Rose. "I guess we just got caught up in it." She smiled at Cyril, who was staring intently at Nick.

"Where's Mandy?" asked Cyril. He didn't know what to expect next.

"I don't know. I can't find her."

"She might be at my house, Nicky. She's done that before. Let's call Mom," said Cyril. "Let's hope she's there. Mom used to work at the vet's office, you know."

Cyril borrowed Rose's cell phone to call his home. "Mom? It's me. Have you seen Mandy? You have? She's there? Is she okay?"

"Gimme the phone," said Nick. "Mrs. Bartholomew? It's Nick. Mandy's there? Is she all right? She ate something funny and ran off. I'm really worried." Nick paused, listening. "What did she eat? I'm not sure . . . um . . . Could have been anything . . . There's a lot of food here." Nick looked at Cyril, helpless. He pointed at the copper plate. "No, there aren't any drugs here. No, Mrs. Bartholomew, really. Does it really matter what she ate? Won't she just puke it up and get it over with?" He listened again. "Okay, let me think, let me think!"

Cyril bit the inside of his mouth, looking from Rose to Nick to Rose again.

Nick continued. "Well, let's see. There were some figs. But I don't think she ate those. And there was, um, a salad. You know, lettuce and stuff. But she doesn't get sick from salad—I've seen her eat it before. Oh, man. What else could it have been?"

"It was whatever was on that copper plate!" yelled Rose. "With that white stuff on top."

"Thanks, Rose," Nick said, then turned toward Cyril. "Oh, right, Cyril, that white stuff. You told me what it was called before, when you were making it."

Suddenly time came screaming to a halt. Everything in the world disappeared except Nick's words and the silence Cyril knew he had to fill. It was all over.

"Um," said Cyril quietly, in a half whisper. He cleared his throat. "Truffles, I guess. With caramelized onions."

Rose took a step back. "I knew it. . . ."

"That's it!" yelled Nick back into the phone. "Truffles!" He listened another moment. "Oh, thank you. Thank you. So she'll be okay? Truffles are no big deal? Okay, I'll be right over. We don't need to call the vet? Bye, Mrs. Bartholomew." He hung up. "She said she's seen this before with truffles. We don't have to worry!" He smiled broadly. Cyril and Rose just glared at him in disbelief. He still hadn't gotten it.

A thick silence hung over the patio as the CD finished. Cyril tried hard not to look over at Rose. He wasn't worried about her being mad. He could take her anger. What he really feared was her disgust.

163

"Cyril?" she asked, staring, fixed.

Cyril looked at the ground. He whispered, "Rose, I'm sorry."

"Cyril? Did you make this dinner?" Rose's voice got louder, and Cyril froze. "Cyril?" Rose's eyes were still on him, white-hot.

"Rose, I—" Cyril's voice caught. He was stuck. He knew it was all out in the open now. Part of him was free, and part of him was dead. His breathing slowed and deepened. "Yes," he whispered, eyes searching the room for something, anything to focus on. "I made the dinner."

"I helped," Nick said.

"You helped? Is that all you have to say for yourself, Nick?" Rose fumed. She collected her hair in her hands, and with the elastic that was on her wrist she efficiently crafted a ponytail, severe, smooth, and utterly perfect.

"I should have listened to Jamie. She was on to you, but I didn't believe her until I saw Cyril hiding in the kitchen." She turned away. "I can't believe you both lied to me."

"Wait, Rose."

"Nick. Did you even make the kitchen-sink cookies?"

"No," said Cyril. "He didn't. I did that, too."

"I can't believe this," said Rose. "I am such an idiot."

"No, you're not," Nick pleaded. "I just wanted you to like me. Rose, wait."

"Don't, Nick. Don't talk to me. Don't call me. You too, Cyril. Enjoy the aphrodisiacs. Which, in case you were wondering, Cyril, don't really work. I was just trying to trick you into telling me the truth about you cooking the meal."

"Please, Rose." Cyril reached out toward Rose. "Wait . . ."

She ran out into the driveway with the boys chasing after her.

"No." Rose pulled out her cell phone and started dialing. "Jamie? It's me. Where are you? Can you ditch him? I need to talk to you." She slammed her car door, still talking.

Cyril stood in the stone driveway and watched Rose rev the engine, and when her high-beam headlights went up, he was blinded, laid bare. He covered his eyes and sank down onto the stones.

Spice-Dusted Figs

2 tablespoons sugar
2 tablespoons ground cinnamon
1 teaspoon Chinese five-spice powder
½ teaspoon ground cloves
½ teaspoon fresh nutmeg
1 package dried figs, about 15

1. In a medium bowl mix sugar and all the spices together.
2. Roll the figs in the spice mixture to coat.

Pita bread

Buy it.

Salty Caramelized Onion Paste with Truffle Shavings
(Cook the onions s-l-o-w-l-y.)
3 tablespoons butter
2 tablespoons olive oil
2 large or 3 medium yellow onions, sliced thin
coarse sea salt to taste
truffle shavings (optional)

1. Melt the butter with 1 tablespoon olive oil in a

large skillet over high heat. When it begins to bubble, add onions a few at a time, tossing with tongs to coat with the butter-oil mixture. When all the onions are in the pan, turn heat down to medium.

2. Continue cooking onions, stirring occasionally, for 45–55 minutes. Onions will cook way down and turn a deep amber brown. Remove from heat, leaving onions in the pan to cool.

3. When cool, transfer the onions to a medium bowl. Add 1 tablespoon oil. Using a wooden spoon, smash the onions into a paste. Transfer the paste to a small serving bowl and sprinkle lightly with coarse sea salt and truffle shavings, if desired.

Chickpea-and-Pine-Nut Slather

1 20-ounce can chickpeas
6 tablespoons pine nuts
juice of one lemon
pinch salt
½ teaspoon cumin
4–5 strands saffron (optional but recommended)
1 tablespoon chopped fresh parsley

1. Place the chickpeas (including their liquid), pine nuts, lemon juice, salt, saffron, and cumin into a

food processor. Pulse until smooth, adding water if necessary.
2. Transfer to a small serving bowl. Toss chopped parsley over the top.

Artichoke Hearts with Mustard

1 tablespoon olive oil (You might need a little more, so keep it handy.)
1 tablespoon mustard seeds
1 tablespoon Dijon mustard
1 6-ounce jar artichoke hearts, drained and chopped into quarters

1. Over medium-high heat, sauté olive oil and mustard seeds until mustard seeds begin to pop.
2. Turn heat down to medium. Using tongs or a spoon, swirl the Dijon mustard into the oil.
3. Add the artichoke hearts and toss to coat. (Add another drizzle of olive oil if needed.)
4. When warmed through, transfer the artichoke hearts into a small serving bowl. Drizzle oil from pan over the top.

Arugula and Blood Orange Salad

2 bunches arugula
2 tablespoons olive oil

1 tablespoon lemon juice

1 tablespoon red wine vinegar

pinch salt

pinch ground pepper

4 blood oranges, peeled and cut into bite-size squares

¼ cup walnuts, coarsely chopped (optional)

1. Carefully wash and thoroughly dry the arugula, removing tough stems. If you have time, return it to the refrigerator to crisp.
2. In the bottom of a large salad bowl, whisk together the olive oil, lemon juice, vinegar, salt, and pepper.
3. Add the arugula to the dressing; toss to coat. Add more oil if necessary.
4. Add oranges and nuts and toss.

Chocolate Bonbons

8 ounces semisweet baking chocolate, finely chopped

½ cup heavy cream

½ stick unsalted butter, melted and cooled

1 teaspoon vanilla extract or ½ teaspoon almond extract

1 6-ounce package chocolate chips

cocoa powder

1. Place finely chopped chocolate into a medium bowl.

2. In a heavy saucepan, heat the whipping cream until scalding. Pour warmed whipping cream over the chocolate, stirring until smooth. Carefully stir in the butter and vanilla or almond extract.

3. Cover and refrigerate overnight. Chocolate will be fairly hard.

4. Line a cookie sheet with waxed paper. Using a melon baller or teaspoon, scoop out into small balls and set on the cookie sheet.

5. In a microwave-safe pitcher, zap the chocolate chips on High for 1 minute or until melted. Stir and set aside.

6. Using a small sieve, carefully dust the bonbons with cocoa powder.

7. Carefully pour the cooled, melted chocolate over the bonbons. Return to refrigerator until ready to serve.

Ginger-Candied Violets
(Call gourmet food shops in your area to find edible flowers.)

1 egg white, at room temperature (If you're concerned about salmonella, you can use powdered egg white.)
1 tablespoon water
½ cup superfine sugar
1–2 teaspoons powdered ginger, to taste
1 dozen edible violets

1. Whisk together the egg white and water; set aside.
2. Mix together the sugar and ginger, set aside.
3. Line a cookie sheet with waxed paper.
4. Prepare one flower at a time. Holding the flower with tweezers and using a small, new paintbrush, carefully paint the egg mixture onto both sides of all the flower petals. Next dust lightly with sugar. Place on the cookie sheet to dry, at least 2 hours.
5. When all the flowers are finished, serve or store in an airtight container until ready to serve.

Dinner serves two

(Be careful what you wish for.)

whipped hot chocolate

The chatty customer finally left, and Alice turned back to Cyril. "You don't seem like you." She sounded concerned. "Something's wrong. What is it?"

Cyril felt wired and shaky, as if he'd been up all night and had been drinking coffee all day to stay awake. Which wasn't so far from the truth.

"Stuff. Nothing." He rocked up and back and up again, a short, staccato rock.

"Okay," said Alice, flipping through the latest *Gourmet*. "Well, then, how's it going with your AICA preparations? Have you figured out what you're going to make at your audition?"

Cyril replied stiffly, "No. I haven't figured out an entrée. I haven't figured out an appetizer. I haven't figured out a dessert. And I don't really care. What's the big deal?"

"Take it easy, Cyril."

"Sorry." He took a deep breath.

"The big deal," continued Alice, "is that your audition is this week. Saturday. Remember? I know you're capable of acing it, and you know it, too. But you still have to prepare. You've got to be *ready*. Believe me. I've seen many promising candidates blow their auditions. The panel shows no mercy, Cyril."

Cyril really didn't want to think about this right now. "Whatever."

"No, not *whatever*. Cyril, listen to me. Cooking isn't like other careers. You can't start when you're twenty-five. You have to take your opportunities when you're young. This is your time. Take it seriously, and do not blow it. You're too valuable."

Cyril just stared at the floor.

"Don't worry about what to make. Just make sure that whatever you make, you make perfectly, with confidence. Remember, Cyril. Butter-and-sugar sandwiches. Make them right and you could pass the panel with just that."

"Yeah. Well, I don't want to talk about it," said Cyril.

"Talk about what?"

"Anything. Really. Okay?"

"Okay." Alice leaned back over her magazine.

"Alice?" Cyril asked. "Remember those truffles you gave me?"

"Oh, I'm glad you brought that up. Toss them, Cyril. I think they're bad. First time that's ever happened to me."

"Too late, Alice."

"What?"

Cyril, knowing he had nothing else to lose, having lost any chance with Rose and probably his best friend, too, spilled the whole story to Alice. He even told Alice about the way Rose had looked straight through him when he tried to say hi in school the day before.

Alice listened carefully. When she was sure he'd finished, she offered, "Do you want my advice?"

"I don't know, do I?"

"Well, I'll give it to you, and you can take it if you want. You need to apologize. Find a way to let Rose know you're sorry, and make certain she gets the message."

"Why? What's the point? She hates me."

"You may be right. But it's not about how she'll

react or whether she'll decide she's madly in love with you after all. You apologize for *yourself,* Cyril. When you say you're sorry, you recognize that what you did was wrong. You clear your conscience so you don't hate yourself. And you learn a lesson. And after that, who knows what might happen?"

"So you're saying I have a chance with Rose?" Cyril's ears perked up.

"Give me a break. Rose would have to be crazy to go out with you right now. What I said was you need to find a way to apologize to Rose, and she may or may not accept it. Do it even though there's really no chance you're going to get a happy ending anytime soon."

"Thanks. Great. My life is hopeless." Cyril's head sank.

"I'm just saying you need to do the right thing. Come clean, learn your lesson, step back. Things will definitely get better. It just might take a while." Alice flipped another page of her magazine. "It's a good thing you've got your AICA audition coming up. It'll give you something positive to focus on."

"Cooking? Positive? No way. Cooking is what got me into this in the first place." Cyril shook his head hard.

"Wrong again," said Alice, readjusting her felted hat, turquoise today. "Cooking is not what got you into this. Your bad judgment got you into this. Cooking, though, might just get you out of it. Cyril, I know you're in pain right now, but your future is way too important to mess up over a girl. Trust me, this is your ticket *out* of this crap you're currently rolling around in. Cyril? Are you listening?"

He didn't answer. He was listening, but he didn't answer.

"Do not blow this," said Alice. "This Saturday is the most important day of your life."

He knew she was right, but he had Rose on the brain.

The next day, Monday, an anxious and impatient Cyril arrived bleary-eyed at school just before third period. After accepting his tardy slip from the vice principal, he made his way to the second floor and headed for Rose's locker. He was carrying a stainless steel thermos, the contents of which he'd been working on all morning.

He was halfway there when his cell phone rang. "Hello?"

"Hey, it's me." It was Nick. "I'm still on your couch."

He'd been there since Aphrodisia, claiming he had a stomachache. At one point Cyril wanted to tell him to get lost, but Mrs. Bartholomew insisted that Cyril let him stay. "We have to take care of our Nicky. If we don't, no one will." She was always saying that Nick would be a grown-up before he realized that he had been robbed of his childhood, and Cyril knew she was right. So Nick and Cyril had spent what was left of the weekend watching TV, saying no more to each other than "Pass the remote" the whole day.

"Listen, Cyril. I just wanted to say I'm sorry."

"For what?" asked Cyril.

"For what? Dude! I've been lying here, thinking about everything. Not just this weekend, but ever since I got back to town. I never thought it would get this out of hand. I'm sorry."

"Have you spoken to Rose?" asked Cyril.

"Are you kidding?" Nick said. "No. Listen, Cyril. If there's anything I can do, just tell me."

Cyril inhaled. "I love her, Nick." He was surprised to hear the words out loud.

Nick didn't answer for a moment. "I know, dude. Jamie told me."

Cyril let that sink in. "Are you mad?"

"Not really, no."

"Why not?" Cyril asked.

"She's Rose. Everybody loves her." Nick paused. "Besides, you two get each other." Cyril rounded the corner. And there, before he was expecting it, was Rose, filling her knapsack with books. "Gotta go," he said into the phone. He hung up before Nick could answer.

"Hi, Rose. Hi, Jamie."

"Hi, Cyril," said Jamie. She looked entirely perplexed. Cyril straightened up and took a deep breath. "Rose, I'm, um, I'm sorry." He knew he was speaking too fast, so he paused, breathed. "I deceived you. But I never meant to hurt you. I made a mistake. It should never have turned out the way it did." He looked over at Jamie, who was dragging her finger across her neck to shut him up. He was talking too fast again.

But he didn't stop. "Rose, this is for you." He held out the stainless steel thermos. "It's whipped hot chocolate. I made it for you. I hope you like it." He held the thermos higher. "Please take it." He tried to smile, but she still hadn't looked at him. "I hope we can be friends again. Someday." His voice shook.

Rose closed her locker and, walking away without looking at him, said, "No, thank you."

She spoke as if he were passing hors d'oeuvres at a party. She didn't even say it to him, just toward him. There was no eye contact, no, "No, thanks, *Cyril,*" not even a, "Leave me alone, I'm not speaking to you." Just a cold, empty, "No, thank you."

It wasn't as if she hated Cyril, it was as if she just didn't care about him at all, one way or the other. And that hurt worse than anything. Cyril felt cold. He watched them begin to walk away.

Jamie looked back and gave Cyril a helpless shrug.

When Cyril went to biology class, Rose wasn't there.

1 cup milk

⅛ cup sugar

2 tablespoons unsweetened cocoa

1 teaspoon vanilla extract

teensy pinch salt

2 1-ounce squares semisweet baking chocolate, broken up

1 cup heavy cream

1. In a small saucepan, slowly warm up milk over low heat until just steaming. Add sugar, cocoa, vanilla, and salt. Stir with a wire whisk until dissolved and smooth.
2. Add chocolate. Stir with a wire whisk until evenly melted. Remove from heat and allow to cool slightly.
3. Pour the whipping cream into a medium bowl. Beat with an electric mixer until quite stiff.
4. Carefully fold the whipped cream into the chocolate. Serve as soon as possible in a large mug with a spoon. If you transport in a thermos before serving, expect middling results.

Makes two cups

no-chicken chicken soup

"Mr. Meech?" Cyril peered into The Meech's office at the end of the biology lab. "Can I ask you a question?"

The Meech looked up from his desk, piled high with ungraded papers. "No, you can't make LSD from bleach and Windex. And yes, you can get a buzz from sniffing formaldehyde." The Meech chuckled at himself. Like most high school teachers, he was just this side of insane. Cyril wondered if it was the years of exposure to students or if it was a prerequisite for the job. "Just a little science-teacher humor there, Cyril. Relax, you look like target practice. Have a seat. Now, what can I do ya for?"

Cyril, already a half week into the greatest test of

patience he'd ever endured, waited a moment before speaking, wanting to be sure The Meech was done. "Um, I was wondering, Mr. Meech. Do you know where Rose is? It's Thursday, and she hasn't been at school since Monday."

"Rose?" The Meech's tone suddenly got unusually serious and he took off his glasses. "She had her seat changed, you know." The Meech glared over his glasses. "You are no longer her lab partner, Bartholomew."

"I know." Cyril lost control of his eyes as they darted from the periodic table to his sneakers to the fish tank to Meech's hairline to the skeleton back in the corner. The Meech was still glaring. "Do you know if she's okay? I was just worried."

The Meech slipped his glasses back on and returned to his papers. "She's at home. She has the flu, I believe."

"Thank you, Mr. Meech." As Cyril backed through the door, he bumped into Jamie.

"Watch it, Cyril!" Cyril spun around. He'd knocked her on the arm and splattered Jamie's coffee all over her faux-snakeskin pants. "Hello! Dry-clean only!"

"Sorry, Jamie."

"How are you, Cyril?" Her voice changed quickly from agitation to concern.

"I'm okay. I'm just late."

"For what?" she asked.

"For Rose. For everything." He pushed past her. "Gotta run!"

"Wait, Cyril. Did you *really* make those kitchen-sink cookies?"

"Yeah, why?"

"They were amazing. Best cookies I've ever tasted. I still think about them," Jamie said. "No matter what happens, you should know how good you are at what you do."

Cyril raced on.

"Cyril, don't do anything stupid!" shouted Jamie. "Or at least try not to."

Cyril was back at home, wrist deep in rings of pale green-and-white leeks and chopped carrots before he realized he'd been running on instinct since speaking to The Meech. He hadn't really thought about what to do when he heard Rose was sick, he just started doing it. Alice's words echoed around him. "Make certain she gets the message."

Her other words, "Focus on your audition. You're too valuable," were completely lost on him now. All he saw was Rose.

*　　*　　*

It was an epic session in the kitchen that night. Cyril cleaned, chopped, sliced, sautéed, boiled, simmered, stirred, tasted, infused, blended, nursed, coaxed, adjusted, and readjusted a vast array of fresh vegetables and herbs, tasting at every turn. He used carrots, onions, celery, bay leaves, mustard, leeks, garlic, sage, kale, and more. The kitchen was awash with the aromas of garlic, herbs, onion, comfort, healing, and love.

Twice Alice called to ask about his audition and whether he was preparing. Twice Cyril let the answering machine take the message.

He went to bed hopeful, knowing he'd made a truly unparalleled soup. And first thing in the morning, he left it in a thermos on Rose's porch.

Rose was wide awake. She could have slept through Garfunkel's panting in her ear another twenty minutes, easy. But the cold, damp shock she felt from Simon's wet tongue brought her to the point of no return. There was no rolling over and going back to sleep after that doggy treat.

"Okay, you two, Mama Pajama rises," she said as she scratched and patted her two cocker spaniels. She stretched her arms over her head and put on her oversized glasses before flipping on the ultimate sick-day show, *The Price Is Right*. But when the screaming housewife from Topanga Canyon priced the Black & Decker Juice Wizard at fifty dollars, Rose was done. It didn't take a professional chef to know that fifty was way out of the ballpark. Even Nick would have known that.

Nick.

Rose was still feeling angry toward Nick. Sometimes she felt like driving over to his house and cracking him across the face. Or advising him via e-mail that the expression is "for all intents and purposes," not "for all intensive purposes." But if she felt like slapping Nick, then she felt like punching Cyril in the stomach. For some reason, his betrayal hurt more.

But she was tired of the anger and hurt and thought fresh air would do her some good. She stuffed some tissues up her nose (always the conservationist, she found that this method cut down on the number of tissues wasted), wrapped herself in her quilt, and headed to the kitchen for a cup of tea to bring outside.

Out on the porch, she settled into the rocking chair that had been sitting there since before she was born. It had belonged to her mother's mother, and Rose couldn't help but wonder if she herself looked like someone's mother's mother—rocking back and forth, sipping herbal tea, tissues coming out of her nostrils—she gave the distinct appearance of someone who had stopped caring what other people thought, the way old people are prone to do. The thought of it made her chuckle.

Just then something shiny caught her eye—a spotless, stainless steel thermos with a note tied to it. *For Rose, with Love.*

At first she ignored it. "Didn't he already try the thermos thing?" she growled, and left it out on the porch, slamming the door behind her.

She headed back upstairs to give Bob Barker another chance, but all the Betty Crocker/Del Monte/Chef Boyardee commercials drove her right back down to the kitchen and into its empty cupboards. A note from her mother telling her to order delivery from the supermarket and a dusty jar of capers were all she found.

The thermos outside on the porch was calling her name.

But she couldn't.

Or could she?

She had to. She was starving.

She brought in the thermos and read the rest of the note. *No-Chicken Chicken Soup. From a Friend.* She rolled her eyes while she unscrewed the thermos. Smelled tasty.

The universe had spoken.

She dumped the soup into a pan and turned on the flame. It was Cyril she was angry at, not his food, for goodness' sake.

As she poured the soup into a mug, she could smell its rich, earthy, robust, and healing aroma. She exhaled, then dropped her nose into her mug to take in another, deeper breath. Wow. Could he really have made this soup? It smelled like nothing she'd ever smelled before, yet it smelled completely familiar. It was like she'd had it all her life . . . or wanted to have it for the rest of her life . . . or both.

And then she raised her spoon to her mouth and felt the soup send beams of warmth and life through her body to her stomach, her head, and her heart. From the moment she raised the spoon to her mouth, her arm was in constant motion. When she'd drained the mug, slurping loudly, she reached for the pan and poured out some more. As she sipped her second mug, she felt the soup traveling throughout her body. It was as if every cell was having a sip and every cell was desperately thirsty.

It tastes like Nick's food. But Nick's food wasn't

Nick's food. It was Cyril's food. Rose soaked her nostrils in the soup's powerful steam.

Suddenly Cyril's image hung in front of her. She had never realized before how many faces he had. His happy face, joking with her in biology. His strong face, listening to her cry about Brandon. His defiant face, saving her from humiliation in The Meech's class. His fearful face, confessing to the deception. His vulnerable face, offering her whipped hot chocolate.

What is in this soup? It made her dizzy and clearheaded both at the same time. It beckoned her to sleep and awaken at the same time. What is in it?

She closed her lids and Cyril's face, his ice-blue eyes, looked back at her. That was her answer. Cyril. That's what's in the soup. Cyril.

It was the last thought Rose had before she slept. And she slept so deeply, she didn't wake up until the next day.

3 full heads of garlic

2 teaspoons chili powder

3 quarts fresh, cool water

3 large leeks, chopped into rings

1 pound carrots, chopped

2 large onions, chopped

1 bunch of celery, chopped

2 bay leaves

2 teaspoons mustard powder

1 tablespoon cumin

1 bunch kale, chopped

2 tablespoons dried sage

1 bag of prewashed spinach, chopped

¼ cup fresh ginger, carefully peeled with a vegetable
peeler and sliced into paper-thin little pieces

1. Slice all three heads of garlic in half. Remove
excess skin, but don't worry about removing
all of it. Place garlic heads, chili powder, and
water into a large saucepan over medium-
high heat. Bring to a slow boil, reduce heat to
low, and simmer, tightly covered, for 1 hour.
Skim off any foam that comes to the top with
a slotted spoon. This step infuses the water
with all the healthy properties of the garlic
without making it taste garlicky.

2. While the garlic is simmering, chop up the other vegetables. Soak the chopped leeks in cool water to get out all the dirt and grit. (Leeks are notoriously sandy.) Sauté carrots, onions, celery, and bay leaves in a soup pot over medium heat until soft but not brown. Add the mustard powder and cumin.
3. Strain the garlic water through a sieve into a soup pot. Discard the garlic and skins. Add the chopped kale. Simmer for 30 minutes.
4. Carefully remove the bay leaves. Add the leeks and sage. Simmer for 10 more minutes. Add the spinach and ginger; simmer for 10 more minutes.
5. Serve hot with crusty country bread. Or refrigerate and reheat and serve tomorrow. This soup gets better every time you reheat it.

Makes two to three quarts

(With sincerest apologies . . . from the nonboyfriend boy friend.)

pear charlotte

"Mr. Bartholomew."

Cyril looked up from his cooking station. The Austrian chef-professor, towering above him—with his perfectly cylindrical headgear, trimmed eyebrows, and impeccably alabaster chef's jacket with green-and-gold collar stripes signifying his utmost-exalted chef-ness—didn't look happy. "Ze jacket. Ve have a problem." He pointed at Cyril's white chef's coat.

Cyril looked down. He didn't see anything wrong. "Yes?"

"Ze button! Ze string!" He thrust his finger at Cyril's chest. Sure enough, the third white button down, in the left column, had a barely perceptible white thread hanging from it.

"I'm very sorry, Chef." Cyril grabbed his kitchen scissors and snipped it off. He'd felt pretty lucky that he'd even made it in on time, and frankly, the fact that his mom had cleaned and ironed his chef's jacket had been a favor sent from the heavens. He felt good about getting away with little more than a dangling thread.

"Hmph." The chef-professor walked on.

Cyril turned back to his station. His *mise-en-place*, his setup of ingredients, was in place. Kosher salt, three boxes. Two whole red snappers with nice clear eyes. A stack of pears. A bowl of turnips, sweet potatoes, taro, carrots, and more. Two packages of ladyfingers. Plenty of garlic, nutmeg, butter, sugar, olive oil . . . staples. Spices were gathered, and water was boiling.

He would have exactly three hours to prepare his audition meal for the panel of five chef-professors, including the Austrian, Chief Pastry Chef Helmut Rammstein, and the head chef of the AICA, Chef Kitty Woo. Kitty Woo was a legend. She'd once stopped in at Oregano, and Alice introduced Cyril to her. Cyril remembered nothing besides perspiring all over Kitty Woo's hand.

Cyril was confident about his salt-baked snapper

and root-vegetable gratin. The carrot consommé was less familiar, but Cyril believed he'd pull it off. Dessert was another story.

He'd considered everything in his repertoire, from the flourless chocolate cake to the apricot galettes to the frozen bombe tropicale. Everything was too boring, too showy, too risky, too easy, too predictable, or too pretentious. Everything except for pear charlotte.

Pear charlotte was the perfect finale for his audition. He could use local ingredients (chef panels always loved that) and show off some skills, and there's no *way* anyone else auditioning would think of it. The only problem was that he'd never made it before. He'd been planning on a rehearsal, but in all the no-chicken soup frenzy, he never got around to it. But Cyril wasn't worried. He'd created a million perfect desserts in his life, and today would be no different.

Except it would be. Today he no longer had even the fantasy of Rose. She was gone.

Stop! Cyril's brain told his heart to shut up. *Focus!* He had to get himself into the zone. It was his only hope.

Cyril did a quick 360 and checked out the competition. There were three other prospectives: one girl, whom he recognized from around the farmer's market, and a pair of twin boys who'd flown in from Arizona.

"Prospectives!" howled Rammstein, shrill. "You have three hours to complete your required three courses. Vun appetizer, vun main dish, and vun dessert. Zere vill be no exceptions. Remember, each dish must be perfect in construction, technique, flavor, and presentation, or your application to the undergraduate program vill be immediately discarded. May I remind you, lady and gentlemen, zat zis is ze most prestigious and competitive culinary program in zis country, if not ze world, and ve expect nothing less zan perfection."

For the first time in the history of his cooking career Cyril felt nervous. Because for the first time he realized that this was indeed the most important day of his life. He inhaled deeply, desperately, trying to conjure up the zone.

"And now, please begin!" barked Rammstein.

Cyril was in action immediately. He began with the charlotte, which would have to chill. He put a cup of water and two cups of sugar in a saucepan, swirling it over the heat until it began to slow-bubble into a rich, sweet, stringy syrup. He took up one of the small

Williams pears, peeled it, cored it, and dropped it in the syrup. The remaining five pears quickly followed until the syrup was crowded. He covered the pan and moved it away from the flame to let them steam slowly in their own juices.

Rammstein was definitely on the prowl. Cyril could hear him across the room. "Randy? Andy? Vich vun are you? Your kitchen towel is on ze floor!" Using his fingers as a sieve, Cyril began separating eggs. He needed four yolks for the filling, and he'd save the whites—if he had time, he'd make a crown for the charlotte. One egg, clean. Second egg, clean. The third egg, he broke the yolk. This was bad—any broken yolk would ruin any chance of whipping the whites. Third egg again, clean. Fourth egg, another broken yolk. Cyril couldn't remember the last time he'd even flinched at such an easy task. Separating eggs was like *Cooking for Dummies*. He tried again, but when he went to crack the egg, it shattered in his fist. Cyril felt a bead of sweat on his upper lip and licked it off.

Watching it like a hawk, he assembled the pale, creamy yellow custard. Using a tasting spoon, he brought some to his lips. Smooth, rich, silky, light, and not too eggy. Satisfied, he scraped it into another glass bowl, covered it, and slid it into one of the shared fridges.

Cyril had about ten minutes of chopping to do for his soup and gratin. Onion, celery, garlic, and, of course, carrots. He chopped carefully, slowly, deliberately. Kitty Woo wandered by to check out his skills. "Nice work," she said. Cyril didn't answer. He couldn't believe *she'd* just said that.

Just behind her Helmut Rammstein muttered at Cyril, "Young man, ze syrup is still bubbling."

Cyril spun around to the stove. *No!* He turned off the heat and yanked the saucepan to a towel on the counter. But the mixture, which had once been clear, was now cloudy. And smoking.

Think. Think. Cyril knew he could salvage this by turning it into a caramel sauce. He raced to the refrigerator for some heavy cream, ripped open the carton, and poured it, too quickly, into the syrup. "Whisk!" he yelled, reaching for his custard-coated whisk. Cyril plunged it into the caramel. The whisk wouldn't budge. Cyril took another look at Rammstein, who was shaking his head and whispering in Kitty Woo's ear. Setting the caramel aside, he returned to his vegetables to think. Turnips, sweet potatoes, parsnips.

Halfway through his second turnip, Cyril's knife

slipped. Knowing what he'd done before he could even open his eyes, Cyril dropped his knife and grabbed frantically at the kitchen towel tucked into his apron. By the time he'd wrapped it around his finger, half of his cutting board had been stained red. It didn't hurt, but the blood was flowing freely.

"Bartholomew!" Cyril didn't look up. He wrapped his forefinger, now a few ounces lighter and a few millimeters shorter, in the towel and walked raggedly to the sink. Rammstein was racing toward him with a first-aid kit. "Bartholomew!"

"It's okay. I'm okay."

Rammstein carefully bandaged Cyril's finger, lecturing him the whole time. "It is very important to vatch ze knife. I cannot stress zis enuff. Not only is it unsanitary, it is dangerous to your fingers and ozer extremities. Do you hear vhat I say?"

"Yes, Chef."

"Your finger vill be okay. And by ze way, Bartholomew, is that a special variation of charlotte you're making?"

"No, why?"

"Because ze charlotte takes many hours to set up properly. But if you have tested ze recipe, I'm sure it vill be acceptable." He turned away.

Cyril, struck to stone, couldn't believe it. *He's messing with me. How many hours could it take?* He figured he should check the recipe. *Chill for at least six hours.*

He rubbed his eyes, sure he was hallucinating. *Chill for at least six hours.*

But the audition only lasts three hours total.

Chill for at least six hours.

No.

Cyril's chef's cap tumbled off his head and bounced off his shoulder and onto the floor at that moment. It made only a *swoosh* as it skirted the floor, but it sounded like a hurricane to Cyril. He was mystified. It was inconceivable. He had broken at least four of the most basic of rules: choosing an unfamiliar dish, having an incomplete *mise-en-place,* not watching the knife, and now not reading the recipe *all the way through* before beginning. He was shell-shocked. Unbelieving. The most important day of his life was now over. And he'd blown it. How would he ever face Alice? His mother? Himself?

Cyril turned off his burners, gathered up his chef's kit, and walked out of the kitchen, leaving his audition unfinished.

No one called after him.

Custard Filling:

1 small packet plain gelatin

1 cup half-and-half

1 fresh vanilla bean

4 egg yolks

½ cup sugar

1 cup heavy cream

1. In a medium glass bowl, dissolve the gelatin according to package directions. Set aside.
2. In a small saucepan over medium heat, warm up the half-and-half until just scalding. Halve and scrape the seeds from the vanilla bean; whisk into the half-and-half.
3. In a large glass bowl, combine the egg yolks and sugar with a wooden spoon until smooth and creamy.
4. Slowly pour the half-and-half over the egg mixture in a small stream, whisking rapidly. If you pour in the half-and-half too quickly, the eggs will scramble. You want a smooth, thick mixture.
5. Place the egg and cream mixture over lightly boiling water, imitating a double boiler. Stir constantly until smooth and thick.
6. Remove from heat and whisk in gelatin until completely dissolved. Let cool, stirring occasionally.
7. Chill for 1 hour. Before removing from refrigerator, beat heavy cream to soft peaks.

8. Slowly fold whipped cream into custard. Return to refrigerator.

Poached Pears:
2 cups sugar
1 cup water
6 small Williams pears

1. In a medium saucepan over medium heat, dissolve the sugar into the water with a wire whisk.
2. Peel the pears, leaving four vertical strips of skin on each, creating stripes. Halve the pears lengthwise; remove the stem and seeds.
3. Place the pears in the saucepan with syrup, stirring to coat each pear.
4. Cover and simmer for 10–15 minutes until soft. Drain, reserving liquid and syrup.
5. Thinly slice half the pears, leaving the best-looking ones intact.

Assembling the Charlotte:
syrup from poached pears, cooled
2 tablespoons blackberry jelly, seedless (Raspberry or any other seedless jelly is cool.)
2 packages ladyfingers
powdered sugar

1. In the same saucepan used to poach the pears, dissolve the blackberry jelly into the remaining syrup over medium heat. Set aside to cool.
2. Using a kitchen brush, paint each ladyfinger with the jelly until wet but not soaked through. Press the ladyfingers into a springform pan or charlotte mold, completely lining the bottom and sides of the pan.
3. Place one layer of sliced pears on the bottom of the charlotte, followed by a thin layer of custard filling. Continue alternating pear slices and custard filling until pear slices run out.
4. Arrange the remaining half pears artfully on top of the charlotte. Spoon in the remaining custard.
5. Tightly cover the charlotte and chill for 6 hours until set. (*Six, damn it.*)
6. Lightly dust the charlotte with powdered sugar before serving.

Serves ten

(Chill for at least six hours. Chill for at least six hours. Chill for at least six hours.)

butter-and-sugar sandwiches

Now that Cyril had blown his AICA audition, there was only one thing left for him to do. Stuff his face with butter-and-sugar sandwiches.

The minute he got home from the AICA, Cyril pulled one of his dad's loaves of Wonder Bread out of the cabinet and lined up all nineteen slices. Then he slathered butter on all the slices, soft, gooshy butter that he kept just next to the stove in a butter dish as old as his house. He heaped sugar on all the slices and brusquely slapped together nine sandwiches. He ate the leftover piece first, open faced, folding it in half and choking it down in two bites without even tasting it. The second sandwich he savored. First he pulled off the four crusts and chewed on those. Next he took a large, satisfying bite from the soft, sweet center. He broke into an evil grin. *I bet they don't teach this at the AICA.*

He was just about to sink his teeth in for a second bite when the back door screamed open and Nick burst in with the goofiest look on his face Cyril had ever seen. "Road trip!" He grabbed Cyril around the shoulders. "Congratulations, dude! You've won an all-expenses-paid twenty-four-hour full-on foodie trip to New York! Let's get out of here."

"What? Why? What are you talking about?" Cyril asked.

"We're celebrating! You did it, man! We're gonna eat New York."

"There's nothing to celebrate." Cyril sounded defeated, because he was.

"That bad, huh?" Nick's voice was solemn.

"Worse."

"All the more reason!" exploded Nick. "You're free! Let's blow this hole!"

"Nick, I can't. My parents are in Massachusetts, visiting my grandmother. They didn't leave me any money, and I spent everything I had on my audition," protested Cyril.

"Uh, Cyril. Gimme a break. Hello, rich friend here. I can handle it. Besides, don't I owe you one?"

Cyril was out of reasons to say no. And strangely, it felt good. "You know what?" he said. "Screw it. You're on. New freaking York. Let's go."

Sure, it wasn't exactly how he'd pictured his first real trip to New York, but nothing was happening the way he'd pictured it lately. He raced through the house for essentials, and the next thing he knew, he was headed down the Hudson by train with Nick.

New York was just as Cyril had pictured it. Skyscrapers, bright lights, beautiful people, and every kind of food anyone could possibly dream of. He and Nick had dim sum in Chinatown, zeppolis in Little Italy, mussels and frites in the Meatpacking District. They went to a street fair in SoHo for mozzarepa, Veselka in the East Village for pierogies, and Chelsea Market in Chelsea for lobster rolls. Cyril was like a daredevil kid at the amusement park, overwhelmed but hungry for more.

They spent the night at some friend of Nick's on the Lower East Side, a girl with two tongue piercings and three Weimaraners. Soon the AICA audition was just a distant memory for Cyril, and New Hyde Park seemed like fiction. But over a perfectly greasy diner breakfast of over-easy eggs, potatoes, and a bottomless cup of coffee,

Nick's cell phone rang, which reminded Cyril that a world still existed beyond this eating extravaganza.

"Hello? Tonight. What time is good? Okay. Bye."

"Who was that?" Cyril asked, mopping up his yolk with buttered white toast.

"No one. How're your eggs?"

"Amazing. Everything in this town is amazing. Did you taste the way they got those picrogies so light last night? But still rich?" Cyril didn't mind that his culinary observations were lost on Nick. He liked to make them, anyway. "And the mussels. I've never had seafood that fresh. It's totally different. And what were those corn cakes with the cheese called? Mozzarepa? Mmm. And dim sum, with the broth inside the dumplings. Wow." He began to trail off, mumbling, "Rose would love those. Too bad she's not speaking to me." Cyril forced a laugh, but even he knew it wasn't believable.

"Don't worry about it, dude," said Nick. "Seriously. It's gonna turn out okay."

"Sure," said Cyril, thinking how clueless Nick could be sometimes.

The next cell phone to ring was Cyril's.

"Hello?"

"Cyril?" It was Alice. Cyril's stomach dropped.

"Alice, I—"

"Cyril, don't say anything. I don't know exactly what happened yesterday at the AICA, and I'm not sure I want to, but Kitty Woo was in the store this morning, so I've heard at least one side of the story. She said, by the way, that the custard was the best she'd ever tasted."

Cyril was quiet.

"Oh, wait, before I forget. Someone else was in today, too. A girl named Rose. I believe you know her, Cyril?" teased Alice.

"Rose? Rose was there?" Cyril looked over at Nick. "What was she doing there? I thought she was sick."

"Well, she didn't seem sick to me. She *was* talkative, though. Obviously a novice shopper. She had so many questions about this recipe she was making. Kitchen-sink cookies. I thought that was funny, because you're the only person I've ever heard talk about kitchen-sink cookies before. So I sort of made up a recipe for her."

Cyril frowned at Nick. Of course. Rose was making the cookies for Nick. That must have been her calling before. She and Nick were back together. She was going to give the cookies to him tonight. And this whole trip to New York was Nick's idea of breaking it to Cyril gently or something. Cyril put down his fork and began to simmer.

"Anyway," said Alice. "Back to the important stuff. I happened to have this extra bottle of wine, a 1985 Côtes du Rhône, on the counter this morning. It's really expensive, and, well, I did a little negotiating with the Woo. She's going to give you another go, on my absolute guarantee that it'll be worth it. You have a makeup audition on Monday, twelve noon. You'll have to miss school."

"What?" exclaimed Cyril. "They don't *do* that at the AICA. Besides, I can't miss school!"

"They do now. It's amazing what a stellar bottle of wine can get you. But Cyril, this time you're doing it not just for yourself, but for me. And yes, you *can* miss school. Cyril, do not blow it this time, or my reputation in this town is toast. You can thank me later. Got customers!" And she hung up.

"Nick," said Cyril, muddled and anxious. "We have to get home." He signaled for the check. "Alice got me another audition."

"That's great, man." Nick put down his fork and checked his schedule. "Let's see, the next train isn't until . . . um . . . five forty-eight. We still have time to hit Koreatown for table barbecue and Mahmoun's in the Village for falafel sandwiches!"

"That's all right, man. I really don't feel like eating anymore."

"But Cyril, don't you want to celebrate? I bet they don't let just anyone re-audition. They're probably only giving you a second chance because you're special and they know it. Let's eat."

Cyril wanted to be touched by Nick's kind words, but he wasn't. He was too angry. Why did Nick have Rose's forgiveness, but not Cyril?

"Dude, I said no."

The only way Cyril could keep it together was by not saying another word to Nick. And Nick seemed to understand. So they traveled in complete silence all the way home.

2 slices soft white bread
softened butter
sugar

1. Spread butter on both slices of bread.
2. Sprinkle sugar on both slices of bread.
3. Place two slices of bread together. Eat.
4. Repeat as necessary.

Makes one loaf

butter-and-sugar sandwiches

kitchen-sink cookies redux

"So, do you want to meet at Denny's later?" Nick asked. He was checking his teeth for crumbs in the Shadow's rearview mirror.

It was seven forty-five on Sunday night by the time Nick pulled into Cyril's driveway, and Cyril was anxious to get to work.

"No, thanks," said Cyril. "Got things to do."

"Not even for a quick snack?"

"Um, correct me if I'm wrong, but we just spent two entire days together, and all we did was eat."

What was Nick's persistence about, anyway? Maybe he was planning on breaking the news about Rose at Denny's.

"But you'll probably want to take a break at some point."

"Maybe tomorrow, Nick," Cyril spat as quickly as he could, making a beeline for his house. Nick pulled out of the driveway, probably headed to pick up Rose. But Cyril couldn't waste his energy thinking about that. He had to focus.

Knowing that it was going to be a long night, the first thing Cyril did was put on a strong pot of coffee. He slogged his way through a flourless chocolate cake (too sweet), then an apple galette (too messy), then a steamed nut pudding (takes too long). Nothing was working, nothing was right. Everything was far from perfect.

Halfway through a cherries jubilee, the phone rang. Cyril was in the zone and was only vaguely aware when the answering machine picked up.

"Cyril! Pick up! Pick up the phone. Dude! I'm here with Jamie." It was Nick.

"Woo-hoo!" screamed Jamie in the background. "It's the Kitchen-sink Cookie Man!"

"Listen, Cyril, pick up! Okay, man. We're at Denny's." His voice got quieter, closer, muffled. "Come down and meet us. Seriously. There's someone here I think you want to talk to. Call me." He hung up.

Cyril looked at the answering machine for a

minute. Why was Nick with Jamie and not Rose? And who was the "someone" Nick was referring to? Cyril didn't have time to ponder these questions. He had to focus exclusively on his audition.

He turned back to his cherries jubilee, which now looked like dried cranberries jubilee. Too risky. Not to mention too showy.

He threw up his hands in disgust. Maybe he should blow it off. Maybe he should just drive down to Denny's. Nothing came easy. Maybe his talent collapsed with his heart. He sat down for another cup of coffee, which he was now drinking iced.

Alice's words swirled through his head. "Step away from the food . . . Butter-and-sugar sandwiches . . . You're an incredible cook. Maybe the best I've ever seen."

Cyril closed his eyes in a desperate attempt to clear his brain. He could do this, he knew it—if only Rose hadn't called Nick during breakfast, Cyril would be having no trouble concentrating.

Another phone ring. Cyril let the machine pick up. "Dude, pick up the phone." It was Nick. He just didn't understand, did he? He never had to prepare for anything like a big cooking school audition, did he? Well, then, maybe Cyril had to help Nick understand.

Cyril ran to pick up the receiver. "Nick, I'll talk to you tomorrow, okay?" Then he hung up the phone. Maybe Cyril was being harsh, but Nick was being dim.

The phone rang a third time. Cyril decided to ignore it this time.

"Cyril." It was Rose, talking quietly. His heart jumped to the ceiling, but his body bound the rest of him to the couch. "I just wanted to say thanks for the soup. Um, okay. Bye. Wait." She breathed a couple of times. "Cyril, really. That soup was magic." She hung up.

Cyril was paralyzed. He wanted to pick up. He wanted to call Rose back right now, even though she didn't say to. But if he talked to Rose, he would start thinking about her. And if he started thinking about her, he would start loving her. And if he started loving her, he'd just be setting himself up for disappointment. And disappointment added to an audition yields a recipe for disaster.

The phone didn't ring again that night. Cyril didn't open his eyes again until it was light outside. He sprang up from the couch and glanced at the clock. Ten fifty-five. "No!" The coffee hadn't worked! He'd slept through the night and most of the morning. "Not again!" he yelled loudly.

He looked around the kitchen. It was a disaster area. There were mashed cherries all over the counter, shredded chocolate on the counter, and a heavy dusting of flour on every surface. Especially the floor. Not to mention a sink full of dishes. Cyril was deflated. Only one hour before his audition, and everything was a mess. And he had no dessert.

He dialed Alice. She'd know what to do. It took two attempts to dial her number, but she didn't pick up. He left a frantic message. "Alice. Call, please."

He bounced into the bathroom, grabbed a tooth-brush. Still brushing, he thought about Rose's message last night, and it seemed like a dream. Did she really call? He walked back into the kitchen and replayed the message. "That soup was magic." And again. Cyril felt a heat surge through him, a heat that felt almost like courage.

Did this mean Rose was ready to talk? Or did she just want to say thanks and move on? Somehow it didn't matter all that much. As long as she felt better, that's all that really mattered.

Cyril ran a comb through his hair, changed his clothes, grabbed a jacket, and found his chef's kit bag. He still needed a dessert, but maybe inspiration would hit him on the road. Halfway there, hungry, he stopped at the 7-Eleven to pick up a Powerbar. But standing at the cash register, he realized that in his morning haze he'd grabbed one of Nick's oversized hooded sweatshirts instead of his own. *Damn!* No money in the pockets, only a tiny, crumpled paper bag.

Stepping out of the store, he opened the bag. In it was a half-eaten kitchen-sink cookie. Without thinking, he brought it to his mouth, devouring it in two bites. It was rich, substantial, sweet—but subtle and elegant. Even after having been stuffed into this sweatshirt for who knew how long.

Cyril closed his eyes and swallowed the second bite. And suddenly the world changed.

Kitchen-sink cookies! That was it! He'd make kitchen-sink cookies for the panel, dressed up with vanilla ice cream and a warm chocolate-fudge drizzle. He could do that with his eyes closed. It was perfect. And he *knew* everyone loved them. He dialed Alice on his cell phone. "Alice!" he yelled when she picked up. "Kitchen-sink cookies!"

"What?"

"Kitchen-sink cookies! They're my butter-and-sugar sandwiches! Wish me luck!" and he hung up.

Cyril arrived at the audition full of confidence. He knew

the deck was stacked against him, but he was ready for it. He stared down Rammstein's disapproving looks, danced through the kitchen like a Broadway star, and went to work.

Everything was perfect. His salt-baked fish was succulent, silky, and perfectly seasoned. The root vegetable gratin was crispy where it should be, creamy everywhere else, and flavorful all the way through.

But the kitchen-sink cookies—the kitchen-sink cookies made every panel member sigh with joy. They were crunchy on the outside, gooey on the inside, and full of flavor, richness, and plenty of warmth.

"I need a nap," said Kitty Woo after sampling Cyril's dessert. This, as every chef knew, was a supreme compliment. Cyril knew he'd nailed the audition. He was packing up his chef's kit bag, grinning, when his phone rang.

"Congratulations, Iron Chef," said Nick. "How'd it go this time?"

"Supermodel," said Cyril. "I kicked ass."

"I know you did. That's 'cause you rule."

Cyril walked out of the AICA's front doors, greasy, floured, and wrinkled. Squinting his ice-blue eyes across the parking lot, he inhaled the cool, clean air and tried to remember where his car was.

Taking the steps down from the school and into the parking lot, he finally remembered where he'd parked—at the far end, in the employee lot. And there, tapping her toes next to her mother's Volvo, grinning broadly, in a big chunky white turtleneck sweater, tortoiseshell glasses, and a perfect ponytail, was Rose, looking much like a pot of gold. She was holding a plate of something. Curious, Cyril took a small step. It was a long walk to get to her, and he wasn't sure what to expect when he got there. She was smiling, though, so whatever it was, it couldn't be that bad.

"Hi," he said, head down as he neared her.

Rose held up her plate. "Want a cookie?"

Cyril smiled and took a cookie. And although it didn't have the depth or complexity of his own kitchen-sink cookies, it was the most delicious cookie he'd ever tasted.

She took his face in her hands. "Cyril. You are beautiful." And she kissed him, square on the lips. Cyril's breath left him and his heart sprang into his head. She had kissed him! Rose Mulligan had kissed him! A *real* kiss. And even though it was completely unexpected, it made perfect sense.

Rose pulled her face back, looking Cyril in the eye. "Nick filled me in on what you were doing." She pointed across the parking lot to the Shadow. He could see two people liplocked, but he couldn't tell who the two people were. He assumed one of them was Nick, but who was the other?

"That's Nick?" Cyril asked.

"Yup."

"Who's that, um, with him?" Cyril asked, trying to get a better look.

"That's Jamie," Rose said, laughing. "What, you never saw that one coming?"

Cyril's head was spinning. "So I take it you're okay with them as a couple?"

"Okay? I couldn't be happier. But enough about them—how'd your audition go?" She smiled wide. "You aced it in there, didn't you? Didn't you?"

"I, uh, well, I guess it went pretty good." Cyril looked at his feet.

"You're blushing!" She laughed. "He aced it!" she yelled over toward Nick and Jamie. They waved back without even surfacing for air.

Rose hopped up on the hood of the car, legs dangling over the edge, and pulled Cyril toward her by his sweatshirt. "Cyril. Your soup. It put me to sleep for a night and a day. And when I woke up, all I could see was you." Cyril couldn't believe this was happening.

"I—I—"

Rose put her finger over his mouth, shushing him. "Cyril, no explanations." She buried her face in his shoulder. Perfect fit. "I don't know exactly what happened or why," said Rose softly. "But I see you now. You're exactly what I need. And Jamie's exactly what Nick needs. And that night, with all the aphrodisiacs? I don't think I was only flirting to trick you. I think I was also flirting to flirt."

"Rose, I'm sorry. I never meant to hurt you or anything."

"No more apologies," said Rose. "From now on, only kitchen-sink cookies." She held up the plate again. "How 'bout another?"

Cyril wasn't sure if she meant a kiss or a cookie. So he took one of each.

kitchen-sink cookies redux

(See page eight. Equally good whether they're for some-one special or from someone special.)